The Stone
of the
Past

Maci Smithers

5th Corner Media LLC.

Perrysburg, Ohio

Copyright © 2024 by Maci Smithers.

All rights reserved. No part of this publication may be reproduced, distributed or transmitted in any form or by any means, including photocopying, recording, or other electronic or mechanical methods, without the prior written permission of the publisher, except in the case of brief quotations embodied in critical reviews and certain other noncommercial uses permitted by copyright law. For permission requests, write to the publisher, addressed "Attention: Permissions Coordinator," at the address below.

Maci Smithers/5th Corner Media LLC.

Book Layout ©2015 BookDesignTemplates.com

Ordering Information:

Quantity sales. Special discounts are available on quantity purchases by corporations, associations, and others. For details, contact:

https://jasonsmithers.com/contact

The Stone of the Past/ Maci Smithers. —1st ed.

ISBN 979-8-9897033-2-6

Contents

For Grandma and Grandpa.
Thank you for always believing in me.

You're amazing ☺

"Time travel is dangerous. Serious consequences come to those who meddle with the course of history."

CHAPTER ONE

The Move

"WILL! GIVE THAT BACK!"

"You can't catch me!"

Our feet pound down the staircase as I chase my younger brother, Will, throughout the empty house. He's carrying his favorite stuffed dinosaur in one arm and my laptop under the other.

"You're going to break that, give it back!" I yell as we run through the living room.

"Only if you say you won't go with Mom to Pinewood Falls!" he shouts.

I stop in my tracks and sigh. "This is about the move again?"

Will stops running and drops to the ground, pouting. He looks at the floor and draws circles in the carpet with his finger. "I don't want to move."

"I don't either," I say, my tone softening. I kneel down and slide my laptop out from under his arm. "But we don't exactly have a choice."

Just then, our mom bursts into the living room, as peppy as can be. "Who's ready for an adventure?"

Will and I just sit there in silence for a few seconds. "I don't want to go," Will says gloomily.

Mom smiles gently and sits down on the floor with us. "I know. But look on the bright side—you'll have your own rooms, you'll make a bunch of new friends—It'll be like a fresh start." She ruffles Will's light brown hair and stands up. "But we really do have to go soon. Do you two have everything?"

Before long, Mom, Will and I—plus all of our suitcases and our pet lovebirds, Mango and Peaches, whose huge cage is crammed between Will and I in the back seat—have all piled into the car and are pulling out of the driveway.

"Bye, old house," Will says, sounding melancholy. He and I both stare out the car windows and don't say much for the better part of an hour.

"Here's an idea," says Mom, breaking the silence. "How about instead of being sad about leaving our old house, we each say what we're most excited for about the new house and Pinewood Falls? Kinsey, you go first."

"Um," I say immediately. "I can't think of anything."

"Nothing at all? Well, we'll come back to you. Will?"

"I don't know," he says shortly, still pouting.

"Oookay then, I suppose I'll go first," says Mom. "I'm excited for the scenery of Pinewood Falls. It was supposedly named after its breathtaking waterfalls, you know."

Will still seems sad. I'm not any less upset than him about moving. I had to leave all of my friends (I didn't have a lot of them, but still), switch schools mid-year and move into the middle of nowhere. As unhappy as I am, I suppose I should at least *try* to act excited about the move—for Will's sake.

"Didn't you say that there was an animal shelter near our new house?" I ask. At that, Will perks up. "Maybe we could finally adopt that dog we've been talking about for so long."

"Yes, that's a great idea!" Mom chirps.

"Really?" Will asks hopefully, his eyes wide.

"Really!" Mom repeats. I can see her smiling through the rearview mirror.

"Yay!" Will exclaims. "Then we can take the puppy to see the waterfalls! And I can take it to school with me!"

*   *   *

After a few hours of driving and discussing our new home, we drive by a giant sign that reads Welcome to Pinewood Falls. The sign is made of gray brick, and it's covered in vines. I peer out the window. We're driving on a deserted cobblestone road that is barely visible beneath all of the moss covering it. On both sides of the road is a lush forest that stretches for as far as the eye can see.

"We're almost there!" Mom cheers.

I press the button that opens my car window. As the window slides open, the sound of rushing water fills my ears—the waterfalls. I have to lean out the window to catch a glimpse of them between the trees. The falls are huge, at least 75 feet tall. The glistening water is a vibrant blue that I didn't think even occurred naturally.

"Whoa," I say in awe as the wind blows my hair in my face. I sit back in my seat and brush it out of the way. I picture myself out in the forest, swaying back and forth on a hammock and reading my favorite book while the waterfalls rush in the background.

Okay, so maybe moving to Pinewood Falls won't be as bad as I thought.

The car turns onto a long, winding dirt road. After what seems like an hour more of driving, we pull up to a rustic-looking bungalow.

It's just about the polar opposite of our old house. The house itself is made mostly of wood, with gray stone accents and a dark roof. There's a decent-sized front porch, and I can see a patio off to the side of the house with a firepit and party lights around it. The house is small-ish, but big enough for three people.

"Whoa," I murmur again.

When I open the door and hop out of the car, my feet splash into a puddle of mud. It seems to have rained here recently. The air feels damp and it smells like pine needles. Gushing water sounds way off in the distance. Birds are chirping, and so are Mango and Peaches, who join in tweeting curiously.

"Shall we go inside?" asks Mom after she lifts the birds' cage out of the car. Will and I follow her up to the entrance and step onto the rickety wooden porch while she unlocks the door with a key from her pocket. The door creaks open and we step inside.

The interior of the house is very rustic looking, much like the exterior. The living room, dining room and kitchen are all one big room. The walls and floors are made of grayish brown wood and there is a loft over the living room. There's a stone fireplace, lots of windows and three doors that I assume lead to the bedrooms and bathroom. Some of our furniture is already set up, like the dining table, a couch and a rug in the living room. Some of it won't arrive until tomorrow. The rest of it is packed away inside the millions of boxes scattered around the house.

"Where's my room?" Will asks immediately. The emptiness of the house makes his voice echo.

"Right this way," says Mom. She leads us to the three doors, pointing out her own room, Will's room and the bathroom. Will hurries into his new room and instantly starts unpacking his boxes.

"Wait. Where's my room?" I ask.

"I thought you could have the loft," Mom replies.

"The loft?" I turn and look up at the loft. I'm not sure how I feel about it. It would be cool, but there's not a lot of privacy up there. And I sleepwalk at night, so the staircase with no railing sets off alarm bells in my brain.

"It's not ideal, I know, but we'll make it work," says Mom, setting the birdcage down in the living room. "In the meantime, make yourself at home. I'll make dinner in an hour or so."

I walk up the loft staircase to my new bedroom. My mattress is leaning up against the far wall, and there are a few boxes labeled Kinsey's Room in black marker stacked in the corner. My light green rug is spread out and my dresser, nightstand and desk are set up against the wall.

"Don't forget you start school tomorrow," Mom calls from the kitchen. Those words almost give me a panic attack, even though I've known that I have to go to a new school for a while now. I'm not exactly a 'people person,' so I'm absolutely terrified to try and make some new friends. I feel so unprepared, even though I have all night to get ready for it. I decide to focus on unpacking instead of fretting over the inevitable.

Over the next hour I manage to get some unpacking done. I set up my bed and arrange my furniture the way I want it.

Soon, Mom calls Will and I in for dinner. The meal is uneventful. We mainly just talk about what we need to get done before school tomorrow—get all of our books and supplies together, find something to wear, et cetera.

Before long the sky is dark and flecked with bright stars. The fireplace is on and the lights inside the house are dimmed. As Mom puts Will to bed, I sit at the dining room table with all of my brand-new school supplies spread out around me. I look over my school supplies list, making sure that I have everything.

No. 2 Pencils

4 Folders

2 Binders

Pens

Highlighters

Calculator

I find myself dozing off before I can finish reading the list.

"You should probably get some sleep, Kins—you've got a big day tomorrow," whispers Mom, who is quietly pulling Will's door shut. I glance at my watch—it's 9:04 p.m.

"I have to make sure I have all my supplies," I say, trying to stifle a yawn. I go over the list again, even though I've already read through most of it.

No. 2 Pencils

4 Folders

2 Binders

I don't even make it past the binders before I start to nod off. I decide that I can figure this out in the morning and head to bed. I change into my pajamas and crawl under my light green, blue and yellow quilted comforter. As soon as my head hits the pillow, I'm asleep…

…Until it starts storming. I normally like the rain, but this storm is *loud.* I lay wide awake as lightning cracks and thunder booms outside. *It'll let up before long,* I tell myself.

But after about half an hour, the storm is still raging on. I decide that just laying there waiting for it to end won't do me much good. Reading a book always puts me to sleep. Why not do that?

All of my books are buried in one of the boxes somewhere around the house. I do remember Mom labeling the box they're in Books and Stuff. I think I saw that downstairs somewhere.

So, I get up and carefully creep down the staircase. I spot the box on the dining room table and move towards it.

Suddenly, lightning snaps outside with a *boom* that rattles my bones. My head whips toward the window and I see the strangest thing.

The lighting outside is unnaturally blue and all striking in the exact same spot. That doesn't just *happen* naturally. *What is going on?*

I step towards the window and try to figure out where all of the lightning is striking, but it's too far away and I can't get a good view with all of the trees in the way.

A map. Mom was looking at a map of Pinewood Falls earlier. She must've left it lying somewhere around here. I look around and my eyes land on a rolled-up piece of paper on the counter. *Jackpot.*

I unroll the map and trace a path from our house to where the lightning seems to be striking while thunder roars in the background. I glance repeatedly between the storm and the map. It seems to be striking about two miles away… northwest of our house… my finger lands on a building in precisely the right spot. I read the name and my mouth falls open in disbelief. No, that can't be right. I double check, but the location is dead on.

Pinewood Falls Junior High.

My new school.

How It All Begins

The birds outside start chirping at 6:15 in the morning. I sit up and realize I'm in the new house. Oh, right. We moved in yesterday.

Then I remember the crazy storm from last night. Surely school will be canceled today. The building's probably ruined and the power's probably out because of all that lightning that hit it. I throw off the covers, slide my feet into my slippers and clomp down the stairs.

"Morning, Kinsey," says Mom from the kitchen.

"Hi, Mom. School is canceled today, right?" I ask, dumping some cereal into a bowl and grabbing a random jug of what I assume is milk from the fridge. I pour it into the bowl and almost choke when I taste it. "Also, I think this milk is spoiled."

"That's because it's orange juice, not milk," says Mom. "And also, what? Why would school be canceled?"

My heart sinks a little and I raise an eyebrow. Then I quickly change my expression to a grin that's not suspicious at all. "Er—no reason! Just curious."

As I get ready for school, I think of nothing but the storm. It was probably just a dream. It would make sense. I tend to have dreams that are super realistic yet super weird at the same time. I settle on that and change into jeans and a blue t-shirt that says Girls can do Anything, tie back my dirty-blond hair and slip into my sneakers. I pack my backpack and make my lunch–a peanut butter and jelly sandwich with a side of chips. Fancy, right?

Before I know it an hour has flown by and I find myself standing on the dirt driveway outside the house. "The bus will be here any second now," says Mom, planting a kiss on my head. "Have a great day."

Mom goes inside and I'm left to fend for myself. My heart starts pounding as the sounds of squealing tires and the bus engine fill the air. When the bus rounds the corner, I'm shocked to see that it's… blue?

I'm thrown off guard by the unusual color when the bus skids to a halt and the door slides open in front of me. "You getting on or not?" asks the bus driver, a cranky-looking man whose name tag reads *Mr. Hank.*

I clamber up the bus steps. "You're that new seventh grader, Kenzie Everdell, right?" asks Mr. Hank.

"Er—It's Kinsey," I correct him, "but yes."

"Same thing," he grumbles. "Find a seat."

I get lots of stares from other students as I walk down the aisle, biting my lip. *Just keep walking, ignore them,* I tell myself, looking directly ahead. I choose an empty seat near the middle of the bus and pull a book out of my backpack. I read it until the bus pulls up to the school.

As soon as I see the building, my mind instantly goes back to the storm. No, my *dream* about the storm. The school looks perfectly unharmed—every gray brick of the walls is still intact, and the light-up blue letters above the doors that spell out Pinewood Falls Junior High are still turned on, telling me that the power isn't out. That settles it. It was definitely just a dream.

I follow the herd of students off the bus and all the way up to the fancy-looking blue doors, my heart thumping against my ribcage. What if I can't find my classes, let alone my locker? What if I humiliate myself in front of the entire class and nobody wants to be my friend? Maybe I should just turn around and walk home and tell Mom that I didn't feel good. That wouldn't be a total lie.

The school is even bigger on the inside. It's fancy, too—the floors are covered in smooth gray carpet and the lockers are all midnight blue. There are lots of plants and benches scattered around the place. There are several paintings of the school's mascot, a dodo bird, on the walls.

First of all I have to find my locker. I have the number written down in my planner, so I find a bench off to the side of the wide hallway and pull it out of my backpack. Number 1796. I have no idea where that is.

I don't want to bother a teacher by asking them where it is, so I just follow the locker numbers. 1500s…1600s… 1700s. I finally find my locker and unpack my backpack. Once I have all my books, I stuff my lunch and empty backpack into the locker and set off to find my first class—science.

Mr. Calabiner's science classroom is number 108. I don't have to look too hard to find it, because it's conveniently placed right next to my locker.

I step into the room and Mr. Calabiner spots me immediately. "Ah! You must be Kinsey! Welcome!"

The teacher shows me to my desk and talks me through what a regular day looks like. He hands me paper copies of my schedule and the class syllabus. *So far, so good,* I tell myself.

I pull out my book and read until class starts. The rest of the class starts to file into the room, taking their seats. Most of my classmates seem tired and look like they don't want to be here. The girl who sits at the desk next to me seems wide awake and ready to learn. She has dark brown hair that's tied back in a ponytail, bright blue eyes, silver braces and glasses with a thick black frame.

The bell rings and Mr. Calabiner starts talking immediately. "Good morning, class," he says. Most students grunt in reply. "As you may have seen, we have a new student joining us today."

Oh no. *Please don't make me stand up in front of the class, please don't make me—*

"Kinsey, how about you stand up and tell us a bit about yourself?"

Dang it.

I stand up, and everyone's attention is on me. My heart starts pounding again and I bite my lip.

"Um. I'm, uh, Kinsey. Kinsey Everdell," I say. The whole room is silent. My palms start to sweat. "My family just moved here from Perrysburg, Ohio."

"Any interests? Things that you enjoy?"

"Er—I like reading. And, um, writing," I say, trying not to look at all of the eyes staring at me.

"Nerd," a large boy, also sitting in the back row, mutters. A different boy sitting next to him glares at him. My face flushes.

"Ricky! Be nice. And, Kinsey, that's wonderful," Mr. Calabiner smiles. "You can sit down now."

I sink into my seat and relief washes over me. I frown when I realize that I'll probably have to do that in every class today.

"Since it's Kinsey's first day, I thought maybe we could do a scavenger hunt around the school," Mr. Calabiner explains. "It'll help her get to know the school and how to get around."

He picks up a pile of papers off his desk and starts passing them out. "You'll have twenty minutes to find every item on this list." And then he says the most dreaded words in the history of words. "This assignment has to be done in pairs, so everybody get with a partner."

I freeze and start panicking. Nobody in this room likes me. I'm going to be the only one without a partner.

"We'll make this a competition," Mr. Calabiner says, only making matters worse. "The first group to find everything on the list wins."

At that, almost every chair scrapes against the floor. Everyone starts shuffling around, getting into pairs.

"Looks like nobody wants to partner up with the new girl," the same boy as before, apparently named Ricky, sneers.

"Be quiet, Ricky," says the blue-eyed girl sitting next to me, standing up. She walks over to my desk. "Want to be partners?" she asks me.

"Um, sure," I reply, relieved.

"Great. I'm Via, by the way," she smiles, holding out her hand for me to shake. "Via Glass."

"Nice to meet you," I grin, shaking her hand.

Via smirks competitively. "Now let's go beat Zoey and Ricky at this scavenger hunt."

*   *   *

"What do we need to find first?" Via asks as we walk down the corridor.

I glance down at my list. "A rainbow painting of a dodo bird."

Via lights up. "Oh! I know exactly where that is—follow me."

We set off down a hallway with lots of painting on the walls. "How are you liking Pinewood Falls so far?" asks Via.

"It's alright," I reply. "We just got here yesterday, so it's hard to tell."

"It's unusual for a new student to start in the middle of May," she says. "School will be over in less than two weeks! Oh, look, here's the painting!"

Via stops in front of a multicolored painting of a dodo bird. I check it off the list. "What's next?"

*   *   *

Via and I get to know each other over the course of the scavenger hunt. So far, I've learned that she has a younger sister, her mom's a teacher here, she really likes school, and her favorite book is called *Like-Minded*, which is the one I'm reading right now. It's really good. I can tell that we're going to be friends.

Before long, there's just one thing left on the list.

"A statue?" I ask. "I haven't seen any of those yet."

"That's strange," says Via, squinting at the paper. "I've never even seen a statue in this school."

"Should we just look around?" I suggest.

"Sure."

And so we do. But after searching for about ten minutes, neither of us have found anything.

"We're running out of time," I say. "Maybe we should ask another group?"

"Good idea." Via scans the area and points out a boy with light brown hair and green eyes. "There."

We walk over to him and I recognize him as the one who glared at Ricky when he insulted me. Thankfully, Via does the talking. "Have you found a statue yet?"

"No, have you?" the boy asks.

"Nope," says Via. "We've looked *everywhere.*"

"So have I," says the boy.

"Maybe we should all work together. We'd have more eyes that way," Via suggests. So we all start speed-walking down the hall. "By the way, Cavan, this is Kinsey Everdell, Kinsey, this is Cavan McAuley."

"Nice to meet you," I say. Cavan grins.

We begin walking through a section of the school that I haven't seen yet. Cavan stops in front of a corridor off to the right. It's really dark and seems to be deserted. There's a sign in front of it that says No Students Permitted Beyond this Point. It reminds me vaguely of something from a horror movie. "Have you two tried this hallway yet?" asks Cavan.

"I don't know about that," says Via, stepping back. "We're not even allowed down there. Mr. Calabiner wouldn't put a statue on the scavenger hunt if the only way to find it is by going down a forbidden hallway."

Cavan squints and peers down the dark corridor. "I think I see something down there..." and without warning, he takes off down the forbidden hallway.

"Hold on! We're not...!" Via calls, but it's too late. She shakes her head, grits her teeth and goes after Cavan. I'm left standing there outside the hallway with no choice but to follow them.

I speed-walk down the deserted hall, then break into a run towards the end. The very end of the corridor is dimly lit, but bright enough to see Via, Cavan and the statue of what looks like a gargoyle of some sort.

"I told you so," Cavan smirks.

Via, shaking her head, crosses the statue off the list. "Okay, now let's get out of here."

I stare at the statue. There's something about it that seems… unnatural, but I can't put my finger on what it is. I should probably go back to class with Via and Cavan, but curiosity gets the better of me and I touch the statue.

To everyone's horror, its eyes flash blue.

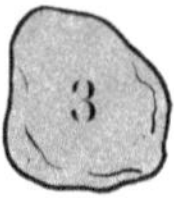

CHAPTER THREE

Into The Past

I yank my hand away from the statue and step back. Via, Cavan and I all stare in horror as the gargoyle's glowing eyes grow brighter and brighter. Suddenly, the ground starts to rumble. All we can do is watch as the statue's stone mouth creaks slowly open.

When the gargoyle's mouth is open about eight inches, the rumbling stops and everything is dead silent.

"What do we do now?" I finally ask. Nobody says anything for a second.

"Wait. I think there's something inside the mouth," says Cavan, squinting at the statue. There's a long secret compartment inside of the gargoyle's mouth and I spot a glint of gold at the very back of it.

"We shouldn't touch it. This is getting really creepy," says Via. "We should go back to class and tell the teacher."

Curiosity still in control, I reach my hand down the statue's secret compartment. My fingers barely graze some kind of fabric-like material. Cavan gives me a little push and I manage to grab the object.

When I pull it out and hold it in my hand, I realize that it's a small golden pouch about the size of my palm.

"What's in it?" asks Cavan. I pull open the pouch.

"Guys… this isn't a good idea…" Via bites her lip, her eyes darting around anxiously.

I dump the contents of the pouch onto my hand. All that is inside is a smooth gray stone.

I can't help but be a little disappointed. I hand the stone to Via, who turns it over in her hands. What I hadn't noticed before is that there are numbers engraved in the stone that spell out '2-0-2-3'.

Via rubs her thumb over the first digit. It changes to a 1. Via drops the stone and throws her arms back out of surprise.

Cavan catches it before it hits the floor. "Weird…" He brushes a finger over the 0, and it changes to a 9. He hands it back to me.

"It's cool," I state, repeatedly swiping the third digit until it switches to an 8, "but it doesn't really *do* anything." I swipe the last digit until it changes to a 7. I get tired of changing the numbers and hand it back to Cavan.

"It has to do *some*thing," he says, examining the stone. "It said 2023 before, right?"

"That's this year," Via murmurs, her eyes still wide with shock.

"Exactly," says Cavan. "So I wonder if—"

But he doesn't get to finish that sentence. Before anyone can realize what's happening, Cavan disappears. Via and I watch in horror as the stone clatters to the ground.

Both of our mouths are open but we're both left speechless. I mean, what do you say when someone vanishes before your eyes?

We just stand there for the longest time, paralyzed with fear.

"What do we tell the teacher?" Via finally gasps.

"We won't need to tell him anything," I say, sounding one thousand times more confident than I feel. "Because we're going to find Cavan." I bend down and pick up the stone. "He disappeared after holding this for, I don't know, fifteen seconds. So that's what we're going to do."

Via hesitates but grabs onto the stone. We both hold tightly onto it and after fifteen seconds of uneventful silence, I feel my feet lift off the ground.

"Uh… are we *floating?*" Via asks, looking around.

"Hold on to the stone," I tell her, fighting to keep my voice steady. It takes all my might not to drop the stone and run away.

Via and I rise higher and higher off the ground until our heads are just inches from the roof. I blink, and suddenly, I'm in some kind of endless blue void.

Before I have a chance to catch my breath, I surge forward, then backward, then I'm sent flying backward into nothingness.

And then I'm falling. One second I'm looking up at the blue void, then it's fluffy clouds and leafy treetops.

Suddenly, I land on my back with a painful *thud* that knocks the wind out of me. Catching my breath, I lift my hand to shield my eyes from the bright sun as I squint up at the towering treetops.

I ease myself into a sitting position and rub my eyes. I've landed on a cracked dirt pathway surrounded by overgrown grass and skyscraping pine trees. Bird calls echo across the forest.

I turn around and find Via and Cavan also sitting on the dirt path, looking just as dazed and confused as I am.

Cavan asks the obvious question: "Where *are* we?"

"No idea," I murmur, spotting the stone laying in its own little crater in the dirt. I reach over and grab it with a dirty hand.

Via slowly stands up and brushes the dirt off her yellow sweater. "Where's the school? We were just in school a few seconds ago."

I get up and look around some more. I spot a small building—no, not a building, it's more like a cabin—between the trees. Smoke is pouring from the chimney and there's a sign above the door, but I can't make out what it says with all the trees in the way. "I think I see a building this way. Maybe someone inside can help us?"

And so we start walking through the trees and towards the cabin, the long grass tickling my ankles.

When we reach the cabin, I read its sign aloud. "'The Cupcake Cabin: Voted Best Cupcake of the Year.'"

"What is a cupcake shop doing out here in the middle of nowhere?" asks Cavan.

"I don't know, but it's worth checking out," Via shrugs. We follow her up to the door and a tiny bell dings as we step inside.

The cupcake shop is very different on the inside than the outside—the floor is checkered black and white, and the walls are teal-painted brick. There are several small circular tables scattered around the place.

"Welcome!" the lady at the front desk greets us. She's wearing a dirty-pink dress with an apron over it, and her gray hair is tied back in a bun. Her nametag says *Donna*. "What can I do for you children today?"

"Hello, miss," says Via, "we were wondering if maybe you could help us out a bit."

"If I can help you with something cupcake related, then of course!" The lady, Donna, points to a banner hanging on the wall. "You know, we were voted the best cupcake of the year!"

The banner has shiny golden letters that read *'Voted Best Cupcake of 1986!'*

Cavan laughs. "36 years ago."

Donna looks at us like we've sprouted wings. "What?"

"Um. You were voted best cupcake of the year… 36 years ago."

Donna's expression tells me that there's something very, very wrong.

"No, that was just last year!"

And there it is.

Via's eyes go wide and her mouth opens slightly, but she shakes her head. "This is too weird. I'm calling my mom."

She pulls her phone out of her pocket. "What? No signal?"

"Whoa! What *is* that doohickey?" Donna gawks at the phone. Via just stares at her.

I can't process all of this. My brain is being fed all this new information but it doesn't like it so it just keeps spitting it back out.

"Nevermind that. I'm just happy to have a customer!" Donna smiles. "We've nearly gone out of business since the Dawhill."

"'The Dawhill'?" I repeat.

"Oh yes," she says gravely. "The hotel brought us so many customers, but now that it's gone, hardly anybody comes around anymore."

"What happened to the Dawhill?" I ask.

The lady pauses and once again gives me that look that says she thinks I'm crazy. "You're… not from around here, are you?"

"No," I say. I'm not entirely sure whether I'm lying or not. "What happened?"

Donna frowns. "The wreck is still out there. I have to look at it every day… such a tragedy. Well, can I get you some cupcakes?"

"Um… that's okay. Thank you for your help," says Via. She grabs Cavan and I by the wrists and drags us out of the cupcake shop.

"Do either of you realize what's going on?" Via asks frantically. Cavan and I are both silent, so she continues. "That stone just took us into the past. We're in the year 1987 now."

"That's the number on the stone," Cavan realizes. "1987."

"When we found it, it said 2023," Via explains. "It must take whoever's holding it to the year that the numbers spell out."

"This is crazy," I say, stating the obvious. Then, through the trees, I see a giant pile of wreckage. It's the wreck of the old hotel that lady was talking about. Without thinking, I take off towards it.

When Via and Cavan catch up with me I'm standing in front of the rubble. It hardly even looks like a building anymore—It's a giant pile of fabric, metal and wood, and most of it seems to be charred to a crisp. I can barely make out a sign that reads Welcome to the Dawhill.

"Whoa," Via murmurs. "What happened to it?"

"I don't know," I reply. "But that lady inside didn't seem to want to talk about it." I reach out and touch a long wooden plank. When I pull my hand back, it's covered in ash.

"Hold on. Are we going to be stuck here?" asks Cavan.

"Well, if the stone can take us into the past, it can probably bring us back to the present," suggests Via. "Kinsey, do you have the stone?"

Wiping my hand on my already dirt-covered jeans, I pull the stone out of my pocket.

"That's weird," says Cavan. "When I teleported here, I dropped the stone on the way. But you two didn't."

"I guess you just have to make sure to hold on to it," I say.

"We should probably get back. The scavenger hunt is over by now and the teacher is probably wondering where we are," says Via. I change the numbers until they spell out '2-0-2-3.'

Everyone puts their hand on it and after around 15 seconds, we start floating. Then comes the same blue void as before, and then we're falling from the sky.

This time I land hard on my elbow in the grass. *That'll leave a bruise,* I think as I sit up and look around. Via, Cavan and I are on a patch of grass outside the school, just inches away from the cement sidewalk. *Thank goodness we didn't land on that.* I see the stone lying in the grass and grab it.

"It's 10:13," Via says, and the blood drains from her face. "We missed the end of science and *all of second and third period.*"

"Well, all we can do is hope we get to fourth period on time. It's not like we can travel back in time and make it to second and third." Both of them stare at me and I realize the irony of what I just said. "Oh."

"You're right, though," says Cavan. "We still have a minute before fourth period starts, we can make it if we're fast."

"Should we meet here after school?" Via asks. We all agree and we all split up and go to our next classes.

*   *   *

The rest of the day goes by fairly quickly. After school, I meet Via and Cavan outside in front of the building and pull out the stone.

"We should take turns holding on to this," I say.

"Good idea. I nominate either of you two, because I lose things easily," says Cavan.

"Me too. Kinsey, can you do it first?" asks Via. I nod and tuck the stone back into my pocket.

"Meet me in the library tomorrow before school," I say. "Maybe we'll be able to find some information on the stone."

"Good idea," says Cavan. "See you two tomorrow?"

"'Bye."

And then I run to catch my bus before it leaves without me.

When the bus deposits me at my house, I walk inside. Apparently Mom has been waiting. "Hi, Kinsey, how was your first day?"

"Uneventful." She waits for me to say more, but that's all I give her.

"Okay, well, we're ordering pizza for dinner to celebrate the first day of school," she says. "It'll be here in an hour."

Before long it's already time to eat. I don't say much over dinner. I don't have to, because Will entertains us with every single detail of his day, from the new friends he made down to precisely how long it took to sharpen each of his pencils.

Afterwards, I head straight to bed, my mind swimming with questions. *How does the stone work? Why was it in a school? What happened to the Dawhill Hotel?*

I don't know if I'll use the stone again. Maybe I should just throw it out of the house and move on with my life. That would be much less risky.

But of course I'm not going to do that. I have the power to go into the past and potentially change it. I'm not going to throw that power away.

I finally fall asleep.

Research

"Morning, Mom. Can you take me to school early today?" I ask as I walk down the stairs, already fully dressed and ready for school at 6:30 in the morning.

"Sure. How come?" asks Mom.

"I have some research to do for a project." It's not a lie.

Before I know it, I'm walking into the school library with Via and Cavan, the stone safe in my pocket. Nobody is in the library except for the librarian, Ms. Peaches, who greets us as we step inside.

"Hello, kids," she says. "Is there anything I can help you find?"

"We're looking for a book on magical artifacts," Cavan says, stuffing his hands in the pockets of his vest.

"Magical artifacts?" Ms. Peaches repeats. "I don't know if I have any books on that. You're welcome to look around, though."

And so we do. "Do you think it would be in the fantasy section or the informational section?" asks Via.

"Could be either."

So we practically turn the library inside out looking for anything that could possibly help us. But in the end, we're all empty-handed.

"Maybe we should try the computers?" Cavan suggests. I walk over to the circular table in the center of the library with the computers on it and start typing.

Magical stone that can take you into the past

The computer thinks for a few seconds, then a message pops up.

0 Results.

"Darn it," says Via. "Well, what do we do now?"

I ignore her and delete my previous search, typing in the words *Dawhill Hotel*. Unlike my last search, about a million results pop up. I click on the first article I see and read it.

THE BURNING OF THE DAWHILL HOTEL

The Dawhill Hotel was constructed in February of 1986 and quickly became the most popular hotel of its time. Guests came from all corners of the world and paid a small fortune to stay in this five-star resort. That's why it was such a tragedy when it was destroyed a mere three months after it was built.

The Dawhill Inn was burned down on June 2nd of 1986. Yet, to this day, nobody knows who did it. Witnesses recall seeing a group of suspicious people enter the hotel just before it went down in flames. These people still haven't been identified, so it is widely assumed that they perished in the fire.

Upon further investigation, police say that the fire was started on purpose. However, the wreck was deemed too dangerous to investigate and was eventually cleaned up in 1988.

So it was a fire, I think.

"Why are you so interested in that old hotel?" asks Via. "There's nothing we can do about it."

That's when a new—and probably sort of insane—idea crosses my mind.

Or maybe there is.

"Kinsey?"

A smirk crosses my lips. "You'll think I'm crazy, but hear me out. What if we use the stone to go back in time and stop the hotel from being burned down?"

The two of them are quiet for a second. "Why should we even care about an old hotel enough to risk our lives trying to save it?" asks Cavan.

"Think about it," I say. "With this stone, we have a lot of power. Why not use it to do something good? Like, save a wildly popular hotel that so many people loved to visit from being destroyed?"

"It'd be really dangerous," Via points out.

"Not necessarily," I say, thinking this through as I go. "If we gather enough clues to figure out who did it, we can stop them from going into the hotel in the first place and burning it down."

"I'm in," says Cavan. We look to Via, who bites her lip.

"I—I don't know," she says. "It's still really risky to use that stone so much when we don't know everything it can do yet."

I think for a minute. "Well, the more we use it, the more we'll learn. Here." I pull the stone out of my pocket. "We'll travel back to this time last year." I swipe the last digit once so the year on the stone is 2022.

I hold it out and Cavan immediately puts his hand on it, but Via hesitates. "Kinsey…"

"It'll be fine," I say. She finally gives in and puts her hand on the stone. As soon as she does, the whole routine starts again: first, the floating. Then, the endless blue void. And lastly, the falling. But this time, we land in the exact place we had been before—on the library floor.

We all get up and immediately see Ms. Peaches at the front desk, looking as if she's seen a ghost. "Where did you three come from?"

Cavan slaps his face. "What were we thinking, time traveling in the middle of the library?"

"Yeah... didn't think this through," I mutter sheepishly. "We should go."

I don't know where I'm going, but I start walking in a different direction. Then I realize that Via isn't following Cavan and me. I look back, and she's standing behind a bookshelf. It seems like she's hiding from something.

"What's going on?" Cavan asks as we walk back over to her.

"I'm in the library," Via whispers.

"Um. We all are."

"No, you don't understand, *I'm* in the library!" She points out at an armchair in the corner of the room. A girl with dark brown hair and glasses sits in it, her nose in a book. "That's me."

"But you're right—" I begin.

"I was in the library at this time last year," Via whispers.

"Whoa," I murmur.

"Now there's something you don't see every day," says Cavan.

"I can't be seen," says Via quietly.

"Why not?"

Via sighs impatiently. "If I see my own self just strutting past, I'll think I've gone crazy! We have to get out of here."

I pull out the stone and change the numbers to read '1-9-8-7.'

"Excuse me?"

I turn around and find Via standing behind me. The Via from *last* year.

"Do you know where to find the book *Like-Minded*?" Past Via asks. Present Via quickly turns away and pretends to look for a book.

"Um… I think it's on the other side of the library," I lie, biting my lip. I need to get Past Via away from us because, for one, she'll freak out if she sees *herself*, and two, I'm holding the stone and I'm going to disappear any second now.

But it's too late. Past Via squints at Present Via. "Wait, you look like…"

Cavan and Present Via put their hands on the stone just in time. We fall into the year of 1987.

"Now that I think about it, I remember that day," says Via as the three of us stand up on the same dry dirt path as before. "I thought I was dreaming or hallucinating or something. Turns out I wasn't, and I actually saw *my future self!*"

"My brain hurts," says Cavan, picking his blue baseball cap up off the ground where it had landed when we fell and putting it on his head.

"So, why are we back here?" asks Via.

"I thought we could gather some information on the wreck," I say, pulling a notepad and pen out of my jacket pocket and starting towards what was once the Dawhill Hotel. I write down at the top of my paper:

The Dawhill Hotel Wreckage

Once we reach it, I have to stand on tiptoes to see the top of the pile. I squint, tap my pen on my lips and click it repeatedly.

"So… what are we looking for, exactly?" asks Cavan.

After about fifteen minutes of staring at the wreck, I've only written down one observation that is not helpful whatsoever:

Pile of Wood

"Don't you think we should be getting back to school soon?" asks Via. "We don't want to miss the whole day again."

"Just a few more minutes," I insist, starting to walk circles around the giant pile. But after fifteen more minutes of useless pacing and pen clicking, Via and Cavan have lost interest and I still haven't found anything that could possibly help us.

"I don't think this is helping," says Cavan, who is now sitting on a burnt tree stump, pulling at a thread on his hat.

"But there has to be *some* kind of evidence around here," I protest. "Something that can help us figure out who did this. Like a strand of hair or something."

"I think we'd actually have to climb onto the pile to find something like that," says Via, kicking a pebble in the grass. "And we really should be getting back to school."

I finally give up. "Fine." I pull out the stone and change the year back to 2023. Everyone holds onto the stone and we fall onto the exact same patch of grass as yesterday.

"It's 9:48," says Via. "If we hurry, we can make it to third period on time."

"What do you two have third period?" I ask.

"History," they say in unison.

"Cool, I do too."

There's silence for a second. "Race you there," says Cavan. He springs to his feet and sprints toward the school doors. Via and I glance at each other, then take off after him.

The bell rings just as we step into the classroom.

"I win," Cavan says under his breath.

"Tardy!" Ricky blurts out. "Ms. Betta, those three are tardy!"

"No, they weren't, Ricky," the teacher sighs. "They arrived just in time."

I see Cavan smirk at Ricky as I slide into my seat. Ricky makes an exaggerated pouty face.

The rest of the day flies by, much like yesterday. Before long, Via, Cavan and I are standing in front of the school, ready to go home.

"I have to go," I say, pulling out the stone. "Does somebody else want to hold onto this until tomorrow?"

"I will," Via decides, taking the stone and tucking it into her pocket. "See you two tomorrow."

"Bye."

I sprint towards the parking lot where the buses are loading and get on my bus just before it leaves. My phone dings and I pull it out. Via has texted Cavan and I:

Meet me in the courtyard at lunch tomorrow.

I put my phone away and read a book for the rest of the bus ride. When the bus parks in front of my house, I wave to the driver and climb down the stairs. When I open the front door and step inside, Mom is standing there, holding her phone. Her expression is sort of a mix between anger and confusion.

"I just got off the phone with your school. They said you've been skipping classes," she says sternly. "Care to explain?"

CHAPTER FIVE

A Friend from the Past

I should have known this would happen. What was I thinking, skipping class to time travel?

Now I stand here, facing the consequences. All sorts of excuses, cover stories and alibis fill my head, each crazier than the last. *I got lost and couldn't find my classes—two days in a row. My teachers accidentally skipped me when taking attendance. I encountered a very angry llama and spent the whole morning running away from it (two days in a row).*

Instead, all that comes out is "I… I can't tell you."

Mom looks astounded. I don't blame her; I'm not usually one to lie or keep secrets. "What do you mean, you can't tell me?"

"You wouldn't understand," I say. "It won't happen again."

"Promise?"

As much as it pains me to do so, I cross my fingers behind my back. "Promise."

"You're off the hook—this time," says Mom. "Dinner's in an hour."

I retreat to my room and sit down at my desk, breathing a sigh of relief as I open my laptop to do more research. I read a few more articles about the Dawhill and discover that it was owned by George and Florence Parkonsville, who became multimillionaires after opening the hotel. That won't exactly help us in figuring out who burned down the hotel, but it's good to know.

The rest of the evening goes by quickly. We have dinner, get ready for school the next day, etcetera. Before long I'm in my bed, staring up at the ceiling, thinking about time travel and the Dawhill and everything. I finally fall asleep.

*   *   *

The next day, I sit there in science class while Mr. Calabiner bores us all with a lecture about homogeneous and heterogeneous mixtures.

I sit at my desk, my head slumped against my hand, and check my watch. 8:19 a.m. Just four more hours until lunch.

After science is my first history class, which is almost as interesting as watching paint dry. Then there's ELA, where we learn about poetry, and then art, which I decide is my favorite class so far.

As soon as the bell rings, I launch out of my seat and walk as fast as I can without technically running to the lunch line. They're serving chicken nuggets and mashed potatoes for lunch, and the scent drifts across the whole school. I quickly get my food and take it out to the courtyard where Via and Cavan are waiting for me.

It's very nice out today. The sun shines across the courtyard and birds chatter loudly. It's a perfect day to be outside, yet hardly anyone besides us is out here.

Via pulls the stone out of her purple messenger bag and sets it out on the table. "I had an idea," she says. "What if we travel back to the year of 1986? Before the hotel was burned down? It could give us an idea of what the hotel was like, and we can look for people who might be possible suspects."

"That's a great idea," I say.

Via changes the numbers on the stone to 1986. "If we're quick, we can get back before lunch is over," she says. We all put our hands on it and appear back in 1986. I almost land on my feet this time, but fall over because of the impact of my feet slamming into the ground. I stand up and brush the dirt off my jeans.

"Whoa," says Cavan. He points out something in front of us.

It's the hotel. Except, it's not a pile of burnt wood anymore, it's an actual building. And it's *huge*. The whole thing is made mostly of wood with dark brick accents, and there are lots of windows. The hotel is bustling with people—tons of people are outside, kids are playing games, and there are more old-fashioned cars parked outside than I can count.

I just stand there gawking at the hotel for at least five minutes. Suddenly, there's a *thunk* and Cavan says "Ow!"

I turn to face him. He's rubbing the back of his head and there's a soccer ball rolling away from him.

Then, a girl about our age with curly red hair and lots of freckles skips over to us. "Sorry about that, I didn't see you there," she says. I notice a pearl necklace hanging from her neck that has a fancy silver pendant.

"It's fine," Cavan grumbles.

The girl looks all of us over from head to toe. "What are you wearing?"

I look down at my yellow t-shirt that has the logo of my favorite fantasy movie, *The Keepers of the Keys,* on it. That movie doesn't actually exist until 2023. Via is wearing a colorful sweater and sneakers and Cavan's wearing a video game t-shirt and bright blue baseball cap. Compared to this girl, who is wearing a lacy blue dress and Mary Janes, it's sort of obvious we're from the future.

"We're… not from around here," says Via, hastily changing the subject. "What's your name?"

"I'm Tiffany," says the girl. "My parents own this hotel."

"Wow," I say. "It's incredible."

"Yeah, everyone thinks that," Tiffany sighs.

"What do you mean?"

Tiffany fidgets with her necklace. "It *is* a beautiful hotel, but truthfully, my parents are only in it for the money. They don't even care about the hotel, or the guests, or anything about it. They just care about being rich." Then she looks at us like she's seen a ghost. "Oh goodness. I've said too much."

"No, that's okay," I assure her. "So what's it like inside?"

"About what you'd expect... chandeliers, fancy bedrooms..." says Tiffany casually. "I can give you a tour, if you'd like."

Via opens her mouth to say no, but I beat her to it. "Sure, that would be great!"

"Cool," says Tiffany. She starts walking up to the doors of the hotel. I make to follow her, but Via grabs my wrist and pulls me back.

"Kinsey, we don't have time for this," she warns me. "If we want to make it back before lunch is over, we have to leave soon."

"Lunch is 45 minutes long," I remind her. "We have tons of time."

Before she can argue any further I catch up to Tiffany and start strolling along beside her.

"So, your parents own the hotel, huh?" I ask, trying to start a conversation. Small talk isn't exactly my forte, especially with new people. I never know the right thing to say. And I feel like I'm smiling too big. Am I smiling too big?

"Um. Yes," says Tiffany, frowning. She starts pulling at a hangnail and doesn't say anything further.

I totally blew it. I bite my lip and slow down until I fall into step with Via and Cavan.

When we reach the antique wooden doors of the hotel, Tiffany pulls them open and we follow her inside.

I instantly feel out of place. There's royal red walls and floral-patterned carpet. There are chandeliers everywhere, and furniture that's upholstered with a coordinating pattern. The place is almost immaculate—there isn't one pillow out of place nor one speck of dirt on the carpet.

"Whoa," I murmur.

Tiffany laughs. "And that's just the lobby. Come on, I'll show you the dining room."

We follow her through an arched doorway and into the dining room, which is just as impressive as the lobby. There are candle centerpieces on each of the circular tables with white tablecloths. Almost every table is occupied. There are fancy sconces all over the walls, and the chandelier is breathtaking.

The rest of the hotel doesn't disappoint. My favorite part ends up being the ballroom, which is the fanciest room in the hotel. When Tiffany takes us up to the seventh floor, which is supposedly the top floor, I point out a narrow wooden staircase in the center of one of the rooms.

"What does that lead to?" I ask.

Tiffany's expression is grim. "That leads to the attic. I'm not allowed to go up there, my parents say it's too dangerous."

"Spooky," says Via. She pretends to check her watch, even though she clearly doesn't have one. "Well, we really should be leaving soon. Thanks for the tour!"

"Oh," says Tiffany. "Well, it was nice to meet you three. Come back sometime!"

Via, Cavan and I go back down the stairs and towards the exit of the hotel. "Tiffany seems nice," I say as we walk down the wooden stairs.

"She did, but she seemed weirdly upset about her parents," says Cavan.

Via pulls the stone out of her pocket, but I stop her before she can change the numbers.

"Wait. What if, while we're here, we look for suspicious people?" I suggest. "People who may have a reason to burn down the hotel?"

Before anyone can respond, I hear yelling from the floor under us. I walk down the stairs and stop on the last step, poking my head out from behind the wall to see what's going on.

There's a large man standing at the front desk, yelling at the man behind it. "This stay was such a waste of money! I want a refund, and I want it now!"

"I'm sorry, sir, but we can't give your money back," says the man behind the desk. He's wearing a brown suit and his dark hair is in a hairstyle I've only ever seen in pictures. I think it's called a mullet or something?

"Why not?" the other man shouts.

"We've already provided our service and our time, we can't just give you a refund because you didn't enjoy it," says a red-haired woman wearing a floppy hat and a blue dress with cherries printed all over it. I realize these are Tiffany's parents, the owners of the hotel.

"Can't you just accept that?" Tiffany's dad argues impatiently.

"Accept it?" the man yells, slamming his fist down on the desk, furious. "I had a horrible time and I want my

money back. I'll burn this hotel to the ground if that's what it takes."

Via, Cavan and I exchange glances. When I look back, the angry man is storming out of the hotel, slamming the door behind him.

"I think we've found our culprit," Cavan grins.

* * *

Later, after we've traveled back to 2023 and the school day is over, I'm back at my desk with a peanut butter and jelly sandwich. I scrawl down a couple of notes on my notepad:

Suspect: Angry Man (Name Unknown)

- Said he would burn down the hotel if he had to. I don't know much about him, but he didn't seem like one to go back on his word.

- Got really, really angry at the hotel owners. Possibly angry enough to do something as horrible as burn the hotel down?

- The only problem is that he was kind of a large man and seemed heavy-footed. Probably not stealthy enough to pull off burning the hotel and not have anyone notice him.

63

I lean back in my chair and chew on my pen, thinking about the scene the man created. He was more angry than I've ever seen anyone in my life, and seemed very determined to get what he wanted. With all that determination, I think he could pull off burning down the hotel if he wanted to.

I finally put my notepad away and call it a night.

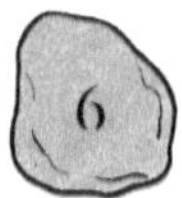

CHAPTER SIX

A Bad Mistake

"Good morning," Mr. Calabiner smiles as students start to file into the classroom. Once everyone is in their seats, he continues. "Today we'll be doing an experiment. Go ahead and get into groups of three, and then I'll explain the activity."

Via comes over to my desk as if we're automatically partners. "Have you seen Cavan at all today?"

I look around the classroom and shake my head. "No… that's weird. I thought he would tell us if he wasn't coming to school today."

Via drops her tone down to a whisper. "I know, especially since he has the stone."

"It's probably nothing," I decide. "Maybe he just forgot…" I trail off, realizing how unbelievable this excuse is.

"Are we all in groups of three?" asks Mr. Calabiner. "Ricky, you can join Via and Kinsey, they only have two."

Ricky whips his head towards Mr. Calabiner and opens his mouth to protest, but the teacher gives him a look and Ricky stomps over to us.

"I don't want to work with you two," he grumbles, folding his arms.

"Believe me, neither do we," Via says flatly. Ricky slumps into the desk next to ours.

"Since we're nearing the end of the year, I thought we could end with a fun experiment," Mr. Calabiner explains. "Your group will have the entire class to create one mixture that's a solution, one that's a colloid and one that's a suspension. There are many materials spread out on the lab tables for you to work with. Any questions?"

Ricky's hand shoots up. "Can I join a different group?"

"No. You may get to work now."

Via grabs a piece of paper and a pen, and our group heads over to one of the large lab tables. "So, does anyone have any ideas for the solution?"

"No," says Ricky immediately.

"Ricky, I know you don't want to be on our team, but can you at least *try* to be even remotely helpful?" Via snaps.

"I'd rather not," Ricky snickers. Via groans.

The rest of the class is exactly like that. Via and Ricky bicker the whole time while I just sit there bored. But before long the school day is over and Via and I are walking out the doors.

"Cavan still hasn't said anything about missing school today," says Via, frowning down at her phone. "I'm going to text him."

"Text me later if he still hasn't said anything," I say. Via nods.

And she does. It's 5 p.m. and I'm flopped across my bed when I get her message.

Meet me in front of your house. I think I know what happened.

"Mom? Can I go for a bike ride?" I call downstairs.

"Sure, just be back by 6," says Mom. I dash down the stairs, throw on my yellow fleece jacket, burst outside and hop on my bright yellow bike. The sun is setting and the sky has a warm orange tinge to it. Crickets have already begun chirping. I ride down the bumpy dirt road and find Via waiting at the end of it on her purple bike.

"Come on," she says. Her expression is unreadable.

"So where are we going?" I ask, riding alongside her.

"Cavan's house," Via replies. I still can't tell whether she's worried or not, so I have no idea what to expect.

"Did he respond to your text?" I ask.

"No," she says. "And I think I know why."

We pull up to a house so boring that if I looked away right now, I'd forget what it looks like. We drop our bikes on the front lawn and I follow Via up to the front door. She knocks.

We wait for a few seconds, and then a woman with blond hair and a similar face to Cavan's opens the door. "Oh, hello! What can I do for you, girls?"

"Are you Cavan's mom?" Via asks.

"Well, indeed I am!" she smiles, flashing her blindingly white teeth at us. She turns around and cups her hands around her mouth. "Cavan! A couple of girls are here to see you!" There's awkward silence for a few moments. Then she flaps her hand dismissively. "I hardly see him at all these days. You can go on up there, second door to the left."

"Did you say you hardly see him these days? As in, today?" Via asks.

"Well, come to think of it, I haven't!" Mrs. McAuley says brightly, still smiling.

"Did you know that he was absent from school today?"

At that, Mrs. McAuley's smile falls. "He was?"

Via glances at me, her expression tinted with concern. I'm still in the dark here. "We'll go up there and… talk to him," says Via. Mrs. McAuley lets us in and we climb the staircase. When we reach the second door to the left, Via knocks tentatively on the door. There's no response, so she pushes the door open and I follow her into the room.

Cavan's not here. Via immediately strides over to a spot in the center of the room, looks at the ground, and freezes. She looks back at me, and then I know.

"It's the stone, isn't it?" I ask. I walk over to where she's standing and look down. The stone says 1887. "You don't think…?"

"He tried to use it but dropped it on the way. Just like last time," says Via. She laughs bitterly. "I can't believe he used it without us."

"That's not important, though," I remind her. "Cavan's trapped in the past. Come on, we're going to get him."

I pick up the stone and hold onto it tightly. Via grabs onto it and she nods to me confidently. Then we start floating, then we get tossed around in the blue void, then we're falling from a dark sky flecked with glowing stars.

I land flat on my arm, and pain shoots through it. I try to use it to push myself into a sitting position, but it buckles under me and I fall back down.

I'm so focused on my arm that I don't even hear Via shout my name. I look ahead and my heart skips a beat when I realize that there are a bunch of soldiers on horseback, all wearing fancy blue military uniforms and sleek black helmets. They march in an impossibly straight line down the path, the soldiers bouncing up and down on the backs of their horses. Hooves *clop* against the concrete at a steady rhythm and the soldiers' chants ring through the air. I can't tell what language it is, but it's definitely not English. Maybe French? Italian?

Then I realize I'm about to get trampled. But Via grabs me by the arms and drags me off the path just in the nick of time.

The soldiers don't seem to notice us, and they keep marching on.

"Thanks," I say breathlessly, standing up and watching the soldiers and their horses trot off into the distance.

"No problem," says Via. Suddenly, she points to the ground. "Footsteps."

Sure enough, there are footprints on the ground. They lead into the woods behind us. And from what I can see, they lead *deep* into the woods.

"They look like Cavan's," I say, noticing the brand logo on the sole of the shoe. "Should we follow them?"

"We don't really have a choice," Via grimaces. She steps forward and starts pushing her way through the foliage. I follow her.

Long grass tickles my ankles, and prickly branches snag at my clothes. I can hardly see where I'm going, I just follow Via's silhouette ahead of me until we reach a clearing in the woods. Cavan is sitting on a log in the center of it. He stands up when he sees us.

"Cavan!" Via gasps. "What are you doing here?"

"Well," he says, "I thought I could go back to 1987 to investigate the wreck some more, but I accidentally went a hundred years too far back. By the time I noticed, I panicked and then dropped the stone just as I was teleporting. And now I'm here."

"You're just lucky we found you," says Via.

"Hey, I was just trying to find clues to help figure out the mystery!" Cavan says.

"You should have told us before you did that all alone! What if we hadn't figured out what happened, and you were just trapped here forever?"

They keep arguing back and forth. They're so busy bickering that they don't even notice the rustling in the forest behind them. In the direction where the rustling is coming from, I see a faint glow in the forest ahead. I rub my eyes and look again. The glow is only getting brighter.

"Guys," I interrupt their bickering, and they turn and look at me. I point over to the glow and the rustling gets louder by the second. I hear footsteps crunching on the dead leaves littering the ground.

I grab a long stick off the ground, preparing to fight, just in case. Via and Cavan step back.

And then, a creature emerges from the trees. Its coat is pearly-white and glittering. Its mane is the same color, just tinted slightly blue. Its horn glows brighter than the moon.

It's a unicorn.

The Hunters

Via, Cavan and I just stand there staring at the pure-white unicorn, entranced by its beauty.

"Is it... real?" asks Cavan.

I reach out with an unsteady hand and slowly stroke the unicorn's face. It's soft like a marshmallow, and she just lets me pet her without even flinching. "It's real."

"I just remembered," says Via. "I read this book once about mythological creatures. It said that the last unicorn alive vanished around the year of 1890."

"That means right now, they're still alive," I elaborate.

"I can't believe it. I thought it was just a legend."

"What do we do now?" asks Cavan. "Do we just leave her here?"

"We can't," says Via. She runs a hand down the unicorn's neck. "My book said that the entire unicorn species will be extinct by 1890. If we leave her here, she could be killed."

"What if we bring her back to the present with us?" I suggest. "That way, she'll be safe."

"Not the present," says Via. "Pinewood Falls is way too populated in the present. She'll be surrounded by people. And if the wrong person sees her…"

"Then what if we take her to some time when the town's a little less populated?" Cavan proposes. "Like some time in the 1980s?"

"Before the Dawhill Hotel was built," says Via. "1984, maybe?"

"That could work," I say. Via pulls out the stone.

Out of nowhere, a twig snaps. Everyone freezes, including the unicorn.

"What was that?" I ask in a hushed voice.

But nobody has a chance to answer, because at that moment, a cloaked figure jumps out of the woods. I stagger backwards, and hastily pick up a long stick from the ground. I hold it out in a fighting stance, and then I realize that this person is holding a crossbow.

"Who are you?" I demand, sounding much more confident than I feel.

"Well, if it isn't a unicorn," the cloaked figure rasps, ignoring me entirely. He steps forward, towards the unicorn, and runs a hand along her horn. "I'm going to be rich when I'm done with you."

"What? You're going to kill her?" Via gasps. "You can't!"

"Yes, I can," the figure says, his cloak swishing behind him as he whips towards us. Via, Cavan and I step back. "It is a unicorn hunter's job, after all."

Out the corner of my eye, I see Via changing the digits on the stone. "I'm going to teleport us all to 1985," she mutters.

Then, the hunter raises his crossbow to the unicorn. Via drops the stone and throws herself in front of the unicorn. "If you want to hurt this unicorn, you'll have to get through me first."

Cavan and I step forward and stand by her side. "And us," says Cavan.

The unicorn hunter grins. "Very well then." He points the crossbow at each of us, one by one. "Who should I shoot first? You, you, or you?"

A crazy idea pops into my head. "On the count of three, follow my lead," I mutter. "One, two, *three!*"

I whip around and hoist myself onto the unicorn's back. Via and Cavan look at me like I'm crazy. "Come on!" I shout. After one last look at the hunter's crossbow, they climb onto the unicorn behind me. The unicorn rears, then takes off galloping through the woods. The hunter shoots but misses us completely.

The unicorn tears through the trees like a rampaging bull. I bounce up and down on her back and death-grip her neck to hold on, ducking and dodging all kinds of tree branches before they smack me in the face.

And then, I feel the unicorn start to lift off the ground. *We're flying.* I watch the treetops get lower and lower to the ground as we raise higher and higher into the sky.

Before long, the trees of the forest are just specks of dust below us. The full moon shines upon us and the stars seem closer than ever.

"Fly, Pearl, fly!" I shout, making up a name for the unicorn on the spot.

"Um, Kinsey," says Via. "I think we left the stone down there with the unicorn hunter."

I pause. "That's our only way to get back to the present. We'll have to go back and get it."

"But the hunter is down there," says Cavan.

"Maybe he left?" Via says hopefully. "I don't know. Maybe we shouldn't go back."

"But we need the stone to get back home," I remind her. "We're going back." I lean forward, pushing lightly on Pearl's neck so that she flies downward, back towards the woods. I scan the forest, and spot the clearing where we first found Pearl. I steer her towards it, and she lands gracefully on the dry dirt.

Thankfully, the unicorn hunter is nowhere to be seen. But the stone is lying in the middle of the dirt, right next to the hunter's dark cloak. I slide off Pearl's back and bend down to grab the stone. Its digits read '1-9-8-4'.

"That's not where it was when I dropped it," says Via. "I think…"

"The hunter used it to travel into the future," I finish her sentence.

Cavan laughs. "He must be so confused right now."

I chuckle at the thought.

"We should really be getting back to the present," says Via. "But if we're going to teleport, we should go back to the path where we landed when we got here. That way, when we get back to 2023, we'll be back in Cavan's room."

I switch the stone's numbers back to 1887 so that it doesn't teleport us before we're ready. Before following Via, Cavan and Pearl, I grab the unicorn hunter's cloak. It's mostly just to have a souvenir of this night, but who knows? It might come in handy one day. I follow the three of them through the woods to the cracked dirt path where we landed.

"Where should we take her?" I ask. "1984's not safe anymore, since the hunter is there now."

"Maybe a year later," Via suggests. "The unicorn hunter will surely be gone by then."

I'm just about to change the year on the stone when I hear heavy footsteps. I turn in the direction of the sound to see two cloaked figures just like the hunter that we'd seen before. One of them is tall and lanky and the other is short and chubby. The tall one points at us, and then they both start running towards us. Actually, I wouldn't call it a *run*. It's a slow jog at best.

"Oh no," I mutter, stepping back. "We have to get out of here."

But it's no use. The hunters have already seen us. They seem out of breath when they stop in front of us.

"Well, well, well, whadda we have 'ere?" the larger one sneers.

"Fred, they musta done some'in to Edward!" the tall one whispers—not so quietly. He points at me. "Look, that one has 'is cloak!"

I try playing dumb. "Who's Edward?"

"You're holdin' 'is cloak," says Fred.

"Oh, this thing?" I hold out the cloak. "I just found this lying on the ground. I have no idea who Edward is."

"Don't lie ta us, little girl," says the taller one. He steps towards me. "We know you did some'in to 'im."

I fold my arms and don't budge. "I don't know what you're talking about."

"Whaddo we do with 'em, Frank?" asks Fred. "Throw 'em in the big house?"

The big house? As in *jail*? "You can't put us in jail."

Frank snickers and steps closer to me. Now he's all up in my face, but I stand my ground and look him dead in the eye. "Whatcha gonna do about it, eh, little girl?" he asks. "Whatcha gonna—"

Without fully thinking it through, I pull my fist back and smash it with full force into Frank's nose.

He grabs his nose and staggers backward. "Ow! Ow, my nose!"

I just stand there, shocked by my own actions. I hold my fist up to my face and stare at it in awe. I didn't know I could do that.

His nose bleeding, Frank turns to me with an expression of pure anger across his face. He points at us with a shaky hand. "Get 'em."

At that, Fred bounds toward us and lunges at me. I dive out of the way, landing flat in the dirt, and Fred faceplants onto the ground next to me.

I scramble to my feet and swing myself onto Pearl's back. I give her a little kick in the side and she rears, but when her front legs hit the ground, she plants her hooves flat on top of Fred. "Owwieee…" he groans.

"Kinsey, look out!" Via shouts. When I look to Frank and realize that he's pulled out a crossbow, it's already too late. There's an arrow flying at my face. I do the only thing I can think of and lean all the way backwards. The arrow soars over my head, whizzing past my nose.

Before I have the chance to sit back up, Pearl rears and I slide off her back. I land on my back with a *thud* that knocks the air out of my lungs.

As I lay there, struggling to catch my breath, Frank walks over to me with an evil grin across his face. "Thought you could get away with that, eh, little girl?"

"Don't—call me—little girl!" I sputter. With all the strength I have left, I push myself up to a standing position and kick him in the shins, knocking him off balance and sending him falling to the ground.

Via and Cavan both rush over and pin him to the ground before he can get up. Now I stand over him. "You lost, you moron."

I step back as Pearl walks slowly over to where Frank lays. She lowers her head and touches the tip of her glowing horn to his forehead. His eyes drift shut, and his head falls limply to his side.

"Are they… dead?" asks Cavan. He and Via release Frank and stand up.

"No," says Via. "Just unconscious, I think."

"We'd better get out of here before any more hunters show up," I decide. Via pulls out the stone and changes its digits to read 1985. Before we go, I grab the other two hunters' cloaks off the ground. We all grab on to the stone, and I rest a hand on Pearl's neck.

The four of us start floating and before we know it, we're falling into 1985. Looking around, I can see that neither the Dawhill nor the cupcake shop have been built yet. It's just a plain old forest, much like back in 1887. Except, there are no unicorn hunters.

"Here we are, Pearl," I smile. "You're free."

"And there are no more of those annoying hunters to bother you, so have fun!" says Cavan. Pearl looks around at us, and I can almost swear that I see her smile. Then she turns and trots off into the woods.

"See you again someday!" I call after her. Via holds out the stone, the date already changed back to 2023. We all hold onto it and fall back into Cavan's bedroom.

"I should get going, my parents are probably worried sick," says Via, glancing at the alarm clock on Cavan's desk. It's past ten o'clock.

"Me too," I say.

"See you later," Cavan grins. "And, uh, thanks for coming back to 1887 to save me. I shouldn't have used the stone without asking you two first."

"No problem," Via smiles. "It's what friends are for."

I follow her out the door and back down the stairs. Mrs. McAuley is sitting on the couch, stroking something in her lap that's either a really fluffy cat or a furry throw pillow. She looks up when she sees us. "Did you talk to him?" she asks.

"Um, sort of," I say. "'Bye, Mrs. McAuley."

We go outside and pick up our bikes. "'Bye, Kinsey," says Via, and she rides down the sidewalk. I hop on my bike and ride back to my house.

*   *   *

When I walk inside, my mom jumps off the couch and hugs me so hard that I can hardly breathe. "There you are, I was worried sick," she says. "Where were you?"

"I went to a friend's house." Not a lie. "Sorry. I should have told you."

"Don't ever do that again," Mom says. "It's late, you should get to bed."

Five minutes later, I lay in bed, thinking. Since I moved into Pinewood Falls, I've traveled into the past, made a friend from 1986, flown on the back of a unicorn and single-handedly taken down two hunters.

Maybe moving here wasn't so bad after all.

CHAPTER EIGHT

Pup of the Past

It's finally the weekend! It's time for relaxation, fun and sleeping in.

Unless you're me.

I'm awake at four in the morning, sitting at my desk with my laptop open, trying to dig up some more information about the Dawhill Hotel. I couldn't sleep after all of the craziness of last night, so here I am.

I search up lots of things:

Who are some suspects of burning down the Dawhill Hotel?

Who was in the Dawhill Hotel when it was burned down?

What was going on when the Dawhill was burned down?

I don't get many helpful results for the first two, just a bunch of articles that are irrelevant to what I need to know. But for the third search, an article pops up. It's titled *Dawhill Animal Week Interrupted by Fire*. Curious, I click on it and read the article.

Dawhill Animal Week Interrupted by Fire

On May 26th of 1986, the Dawhill Hotel began its first ever Animal Appreciation Week. Animals ranging from domesticated dogs to poisonous king cobras were brought to the hotel for tourists to learn about and admire.

Animal Appreciation Week was a huge success for the hotel. But on June 2nd, just as the pet owners were packing up the animals to go back to their homes, the hotel burst into flames. Most of the animals were rescued, except for one young Jack Russell Terrier puppy. He mysteriously disappeared at the time of the fire and was presumed dead.

My heart sinks. I'm sad for the dog and mad at the pet owners for leaving a puppy in a burning building all at the same time. But I have bigger things to worry about, so I try to take my mind off of it.

Today is May 26th. That means that we only have a week until the anniversary of the burning of the Dawhill Hotel. One week from today, we'll have to travel into the past and stop the hotel from being destroyed. Even though it should be easy, the thought still makes me shudder.

We have to figure out for sure who burned down the hotel, or else we won't be able to carry out our plan of stopping them from burning it down.

I know what I'll be doing today.

I pull out my phone and text Via and Cavan: Meet me in front of my house.

It takes a minute for Via to respond:

Kinsey, it's 4 in the morning.

Oh. I forgot. I text back:

Meet me here at noon!

A few hours later, we stand in front of my house, the stone held out in my hand.

"We only have a week to figure out who burned down the hotel," I explain. "We need to find the culprit before it's too late."

I change the digits on the stone so that they spell out '1-9-8-6'. Via and Cavan put their hands on the stone and we land in 1986.

Before I've even had the chance to stand up, I hear footsteps.

"Kinsey! Via! Cavan!" Tiffany yells, jogging over to us. "Where did you guys come from? And why are you on the ground?"

I quickly stand up and fold my arms, trying to look natural and not like I just fell out of the sky. "Oh, you know. Reasons that are totally not suspicious at all whatsoever."

"Okay then," says Tiffany. "Come on. I want to show you something."

She turns and skips off towards the hotel. Cavan elbows me and I shrug.

We follow Tiffany into the hotel lobby, and I'm instantly bombarded with noise. There are people laughing and talking loudly—but what piques my interest most are all of the animal noises—barks and hoots and hollers; things you would expect to hear in a zoo.

"It's Animal Appreciation Week!" Tiffany chirps. "Come on, I'll show you the animals."

She grabs my wrist and pulls me over to a row of cages. Most of them seem way too small for the animals inside. *This is what they call 'animal appreciation'?* I think.

Tiffany leads us down the row, pointing out each animal as we go. "This is a toucan. Its beak is so colorful, right? And this is an otter. Isn't it just adorable? Ooh, and here's the tarantula…"

By the time we get to the end, I've sort of stopped paying attention to Tiffany's comments. But when she shows us the last one, I perk up.

"And this is a Jack Russell terrier. Not very exciting, but he's kinda cute."

I kneel down to the cage and my heart melts. There's a wiry-haired, brown and white puppy laying inside that's almost small enough to fit in my hands. His tail starts wagging and he walks over to the front of his cage when he sees me. He puts his paw in between the bars of the cage. I smile and pet it gently.

"Is this dog for sale?" I ask without thinking.

Tiffany laughs as if it's the dumbest question she's ever heard. "No, silly! The animals are for display only."

The words *for display only* don't sit well with me. In my opinion, animals are living, breathing beings that don't deserve the treatment that these ones are getting. And to think... This poor puppy is going to be left abandoned in a burning building. Too bad I can't do anything about it.

Can I?

"You're welcome to pet them," says Tiffany. "Just don't take them out of their cages."

I nod absently, still tickling the puppy's paw.

"Tiffany!" a man shouts. "Time to mop the floors!"

Tiffany scowls. "I have to go. Bye, guys." She raises her voice to a shout as she walks away. "Coming, Father!"

"Kinsey?" says Via. "You seem awfully focused on that dog."

"Huh? Oh. Yeah." I tear my gaze away from the dog, stand up and turn around to face them. "I need to tell you something. Come with me."

I lead them to a deserted corner of the lobby. I glance around to make sure that nobody can hear us and drop my voice to a whisper. "I was researching the hotel this morning," I tell them. "I found out that every animal makes it out alive, except for the Jack Russell puppy back there. According to what I read, he mysteriously disappears."

"Ooh, spooky," says Cavan.

"He was apparently presumed dead, but nobody knows what *really* happened to him," I continue. "So, either he disappears because he dies in the fire, or he disappears because of us." I pull out the stone for effect.

"What are you saying?" Via asks skeptically.

"I'm saying that the puppy is going to vanish either way," I explain. "And if we don't somehow save him and become the reason for his disappearance, then he'll vanish because of something else. Like perishing in the fire."

"So we could potentially save his life," Cavan elaborates.

"Exactly."

"Well, how are we supposed to save him? He's locked up in a cage," says Via.

"There's a lock on that cage," I say, "and for every lock, there's a key."

"How do we find the key? It could be anywhere in this whole hotel," says Via, sweeping her arm around the room. "We couldn't even begin to—"

"Found it," Cavan interjects. He points to a tall woman in an army-green uniform who is talking to a customer, absently swinging a ring of keys around her finger.

"Oh. Okay then," Via shrugs.

"How will we get them from her, though?" I question.

Cavan taps his chin thoughtfully. "Follow my lead," he says. Before either of us can argue, he starts walking towards the woman with the keys. Via and I follow him.

"Excuse me," says Cavan. The woman turns toward him, looking bored and still swinging the keys. I read her nametag—*Ms. Helen.* Cavan continues. "There's an animal that got out of its cage. I think it was a monkey?"

"We don't have any monkeys," Ms. Helen deadpans, her tone as bored as her expression.

"Oh. My bad. It was a koala," Cavan corrects himself.

"We   don't   have   any   of   those."

Cavan slaps his face. "Sorry, I meant… um… a… guinea pig. You have those, right?"

Ms. Helen's expression changes and she cranes her neck to look outside for the so-called guinea pig. "Hey! You get back here, Gerald!" She drops the keys on the table next to her and rushes out the doors.

Cavan picks up the ring of keys and does a quick little bow. He hands them to me and I bend down to the Jack Russell's cage. The puppy perks up when he sees me.

"Okay then… just gotta figure out which key unlocks your cage and then you'll be free," I tell him. There are around 20 keys here. I choose a key on the keyring and try to stick it in the lock. It doesn't fit. "This may be a little harder than I thought."

I decide to just try them all one by one. The next one doesn't work. I try the one after that—it doesn't fit either.

"Kinsey, that lady will be back soon," says Via. I bite my lip and keep on trying keys.

"She's coming in," says Cavan. I glance over my shoulder, and sure enough, Ms. Helen is walking back inside, having apparently figured out that there is no escaped guinea pig.

There's only one key left. I jam it into the lock and—how ironic—it fits. Relief washes over me as the lock clicks and the cage door swings open. I pick up the puppy and stand up.

"Perfect," I smile. I pull out the stone. "Now to bring him back to the future." I turn back to Via and Cavan.

I freeze when I realize that Ms. Helen is standing right in front of me, hands on her hips. "Put down the dog," she says sternly.

I look to Via and Cavan for backup, but they look just as helpless as I am. Everything is frozen except for the puppy squirming in my arm.

My fingers fumble with the stone behind my back and I come up with a plan. A risky one, but it's a plan. And it's the only hope we have left.

The puppy still in my arms, I dodge Ms. Helen and make a mad dash for the door.

"Hey! You get back here!" Ms. Helen shouts. I look over my shoulder for long enough to see that she starts running after me, but she trips on her untied shoelaces and goes toppling to the ground. That will buy me some time.

I sprint out the open doors and onto the freshly mown front lawn. I pause, adjust my grip around the puppy, and look around. *Should I go into the woods?* I wonder. *No, I'll definitely get myself lost if I do that…*

I don't have much time to think because Ms. Helen appears in the doorway, searching for me. I bolt to the side of the hotel, swerving left and right to dodge tourists who are hanging out outside.

I lean against the side of the building, out of breath, and look over to my side. Ms. Helen is looking for me, but she hasn't spotted me yet. I creep along the side of the hotel, trying not to let my footsteps crunch on the grass.

But suddenly the puppy lets out a high-pitched bark, and Ms. Helen's head whips in my direction. *Shoot.*

She starts running after me, and I want to give up and just let her catch me. But I can't. For this puppy's sake. I force my feet to move and dash towards the back of the hotel.

There's nowhere to hide back here. I frantically whip my head back and forth, looking for some way to escape. My eyes land on an open window. *Jackpot.* It's low to the ground, so I swing one leg over the wall and climb back into the hotel.

I crouch down and peek back out the window just as Ms. Helen runs right past me. I sink to the ground and grin. The puppy licks my chin and I laugh.

I realize I'm in the main dining room. Since Tiffany showed us around, I know my way back to the lobby. I find Via and Cavan standing at the door, presumably looking for me outside. I walk up behind them and tap them both on the shoulder. They whirl around and I hold out the stone.

"Let's get back to 2023 before that lady comes back," I say. I change the numbers and grip the stone with one hand and hold the puppy with the other.

I hold the puppy tightly as we start floating, then we surge through the blue void and fall onto the ground in front of my house.

I let the puppy go, and he hops off my lap. He clumsily begins to wander around, his nose in the air, sniffing out his new surroundings. A butterfly flutters by, and he bats at it playfully. My smile is threatening to split my face in two.

"So, now that we saved him, what are we going to do with him?" asks Via. "I mean, unless one of us is able to adopt him, then he'll have to go to an animal shelter."

I can't say I hadn't thought of this. "My mom has been looking into getting a dog for a long time now," I tell them. I scoop up the puppy, and walk over to the front door of my house. I knock, even though I have the key to unlock it.

Mom opens the door, and she pauses. She glances back and forth between me and the puppy. "Who's this?" she asks, reaching out to pat him on the head.

"I found this puppy walking around outside," I lie. Hey, what am I supposed to tell her? That I time traveled back into 1986 and stole this puppy? I don't think so. "Can we keep him?"

"He didn't have a collar?" Mom asks. "He was just walking around in the woods?"

"Pretty much."

Mom considers it for a minute. "We'll have to check to see if he has an owner first, and take him to the vet, and take a trip to the pet store… but we have time, so I don't see why not."

I refrain from jumping up and down and doing a happy dance. "Hey, Will!" I shout into the house. "We got a dog!"

I immediately hear Will come running. I wave over my shoulder at Via and Cavan, who are getting on their bikes to leave, and bring the puppy into his new home.

Later that night, we take a trip to the Pinewood Falls Veterinary Clinic, where we receive the best possible news—the puppy is perfectly healthy. After the vet catches him up on his shots, he's in perfect condition for us to adopt.

After that, we go to the pet store and pick out all of the basic things that the puppy will need—food, a bed, a harness, etcetera. We even let him pick out his own toys by sniffing the ones that he likes. He ends up sniffing just about every single one of them, so now we have a cart overflowing with various squeaky toys and tennis balls.

"The last thing we need is a collar and a tag," says Mom, looking down at the list that I put together earlier, "which means we'll need to choose a name for the dog."

I'm way ahead of her. "Ropher," I say immediately. It's the name of my favorite character from my favorite sci-fi book. The real dog also looks like a Ropher to me.

"Rover?" Mom repeats.

"No, *Ropher,*" I tell her firmly.

"That's a perfect name!" Will exclaims, dancing around in a circle.

"Okay then. Ropher it is," says Mom. Ropher wags his tail.

Later, Will and I are sitting on the floor of my bedroom, playing with Ropher. Will throws his bright blue tennis ball across the room and the puppy scampers after it. We both laugh.

"Is having a dog everything you hoped and dreamed it would be?" I ask.

"Yes!" Will exclaims. Ropher scurries over to us and jumps on Will, attacking him with licks. Will falls backward and bursts into a fit of laughter.

I go to bed that night with Ropher at my feet and drift off to sleep.

CHAPTER NINE

The Last Day of School

The next few days pass by uneventfully. We've traveled into the past multiple times and found several possible suspects who could have started the fire. Nobody is a perfect match, but they're all possibilities.

"So, we have Lorenzo, the chef with a grudge against Tiffany's dad," I read off my notepad, pacing back and forth in front of the Dawhill wreck.

"But why would he voluntarily choose to work at the hotel and then burn it down?" asks Via. "Something doesn't add up there."

"You're right," I say. "But we also have Rob, the owner of a rival hotel who's always hated Tiffany's parents."

"But it's just a bit of friendly competition. He didn't hate them enough to do something like burn down the entire hotel." Via sighs. "Kinsey, this is pointless. None of these people make sense."

"There has to be something I'm missing," I say, chewing on my pen. "Somebody burned down the hotel *on purpose*. That means somebody had a reason to burn it down. We have to figure out *who*."

"Tomorrow's the last day of school," Cavan states. "After that, we only have one day to figure it out. I don't think that's enough time."

"Or maybe it's exactly enough time. We just have to go back to 1986 and find someone who—"

"But we only have one chance to save the hotel," Via interrupts. "If we rush the process and jump to conclusions too early, we might have the wrong person and ruin our chances."

"We'll figure it out," I say. "We just have to put in the work and then we'll figure it out."

Cavan glances at his watch. "It's 8:43. Class starts in two minutes, we should probably get back to the present."

"Fine."

*   *   *

The next day, there's a feeling of cheerfulness in the air—it's the last day of school. It's so hot outside that nearly everybody is wearing t-shirts and shorts and the air conditioning is on full blast. The bright morning sun streams in through the blinds, and the science classroom smells strongly of sunscreen.

"Morning, class!" Mr. Calabiner exclaims, clapping his hands together. "As you know, it's the last day of school, so the whole seventh grade is going to be taking a field trip to the park. Take a minute to gather your things and then we'll head out!"

Before long, the entire seventh grade—which is about 50 students in total—is walking down the sidewalk towards the park. Many people are walking in clumps with all of their friends, which makes it hard for me to push through the crowd and find Via and Cavan.

101

"I think we should go back to 1986 when we get to the park," I say immediately, much louder than I intended to be. Ricky, who is walking near us, turns in our direction.

"Go back to 1986?" he gapes at me. "Have you found a way to time travel?"

"Wha—? No, no, no, that's not—" I begin.

Ricky snickers. "I didn't think so. Gee, you've got screws loose, new girl."

I feel my face go red and ball my hands into fists at my sides. I open my mouth to fight back, but Cavan grabs my wrist.

"Kinsey, he's not worth it," he says. "Come on." He drags me up to the front of the line, away from Ricky. I'm sort of relieved, because I probably would have just made an even bigger fool of myself.

"As I was saying, I think we should go back to 1986," I tell Cavan and Via, my voice much quieter this time.

"Well, I have to disagree," says Via. "We've been to the past so much lately. I doubt we'll be able to figure out any more than we already have."

"But after today, we only have one more day to figure out who destroyed the hotel," I protest. "We're running out of time."

"Then we'll do it after school," she decides. "But can you do me a favor and try to stop thinking about the hotel for a couple of hours so that you can actually enjoy yourself on this field trip?"

"Fine," I say.

Soon, we reach the entrance to the park. There's a playground, a huge, freshly-mown field, and dozens of picnic tables shaded by large weeping willow trees.

Everyone is talking, so Mr. Calabiner has to shout to be heard over them. "Attention, students! You have access to the playground, field and picnic area for now. We'll play a game of dodgeball in an hour, but for now, go wild."

At that, the crowd of seventh graders disperses. Some chase each other on the field, others stand around and do nothing (i.e. Ricky), and a few goof off with their friends on the playground. Via sits at one of the picnic tables reading a book. I find a shady spot nearby under a willow tree and sit against its trunk.

I know I agreed not to think about the hotel on this field trip, but I have nothing else to do, and it's just too tempting. I pull out my notepad and go over my notes again.

One possible suspect catches my eye that hasn't before—Tiffany's dad, one of the owners of the hotel. He's seemed very on edge to me lately, and now that I think about it, I have overheard him get mad a lot for no real reason. Like two days ago, when he yelled at one of the waiters for adding pickles to a burger when the customer didn't want pickles. If something bigger were to happen that upset him, who knows what he would do? Burn down the hotel, maybe?

I'd say it's worth looking into. I know I shouldn't, but I pull out the stone. I have a whole hour of free time before the dodgeball game; nobody would even notice I'm gone. What could possibly go wrong?

Answer: everything.

As I move my hand to change the stone's digits, a large shadow comes over me. I assume it's just the clouds covering the sun. But when an enormous hand snatches the stone right out of my grasp, I realize it's worse. Much, much worse.

I look up to see Ricky standing over me, turning the stone over in his hands.

"What is this thing?" he asks.

"Ricky, give that back," I say, trying to keep as calm as possible.

And then he does the worst thing he could possibly do. He starts rapidly swiping at the stone's numbers. "Ooh, that's cool."

"Put that down *now.*"

"Why? Why is this rock so important to you?" Ricky questions.

"It's… um…" I grapple for words.

"Tell me or—" For a fraction of a second, his expression flips to pure shock. He throws the stone, and then he vanishes.

I just sit there, staring at the stone with eyes as wide as saucers. I crawl over to the stone and tentatively turn it over to read the numbers.

Only, there aren't numbers. There are words. And they read 'Mesozoic Era'.

I drop the stone as the truth sets in. Ricky just got himself teleported back to the time of *dinosaurs,* and I'm the only one who knows how to save him. This is bad. This is really bad.

I flip through the digits on the stone, realizing that before the year 0000, there are different eras rather than numbers: Bronze Age, Iron Age, etcetera. I quickly change the date on the stone back to 2023 so that I can put the stone in my pocket and tread over to the picnic table where Via is sitting.

"We have a problem," I tell her.

Via hardly looks up from her book. "What kind of problem?" she asks, clearly not paying full attention.

"A Ricky problem." At that, she looks up. I continue, talking fast, words spilling out of my mouth. "I was holding the stone, and all of the sudden, he walked over and snatched it out of my hands. He time traveled, and dropped the stone, and when I looked at it, it said 'Mesozoic Era'. So now Ricky is stuck and we'll have to go and get him and it's really really dangerous and—"

"Hold on, slow down," Via interrupts, closing her book. "Why were you holding the stone? Were you planning to go into the past alone? I thought we agreed not to do that."

"That's not important," I say. "We need to go save Ricky."

"Go save Ricky?" Cavan asks skeptically, walking up to the table. "What's going on?"

"Kinsey let Ricky have the stone and he got himself teleported back to the Mesozoic Era," says Via.

"So we need to go save him?" Cavan guesses, and then he sighs. "Using our free time to save the most annoying person on earth from dinosaurs. Sounds like fun."

"Well, we can't just leave him there," I say, whipping out the stone. Before I have a chance to change the numbers, another hand swoops in and plucks it right out of my hands.

"Ooh, cool, a magic stone!" an unfamiliar voice says. I turn to see a boy that I recognize as one of Ricky's friends. I think his name was Felix?

"Hey, give that back!" I bark.

"So this thing is valuable, huh?" says Felix, checking out the stone. His face lights up. "Ooh, I know!" he turns around and cups his hands around his mouth to yell. "We're starting the dodgeball game early! The grand prize is a magical rock!"

I freeze as he runs off to the field, where all of the students are gathering for the dodgeball game. "We have to get that stone back," I utter.

I march off to the field and right up to Felix. "You can't just steal other people's belongings and offer them up as a prize for winning a game. Now give me that stone back," I demand, holding out my hand impatiently.

"Sorry, no can do," he smirks. "If you want it, you'll have to win it back. So, you playing or not?"

I turn to where everyone is gathering for the dodgeball game. Almost all of the seventh graders are playing.

I gulp. I've never won a dodgeball game in my life. Or any sort of sports game before, for that matter. I always end up losing in the most humiliating way possible. Whether it's trying to use my face as a tennis racket and forfeiting because of a bloody nose or falling asleep in the middle of the soccer field (don't ask how that happened), I always make a fool of myself. And dodgeball is no exception.

I start to reconsider. Should I really risk embarrassing myself just to save Ricky? He's been nothing but a jerk to me ever since I moved here. And it's his own fault that he decided to take the stone from me. Part of me wants him to suffer the consequences.

But the other part of me says that I should save him. He didn't know that the stone could take him into the past. Nobody really deserves to be trapped with a bunch of dinosaurs, no matter how rude they are. Plus, that stone is key to solving the mystery of the Dawhill Hotel, and potentially saving it.

"Fine," I decide. "I'll play."

"And I will too," says Cavan as he and Via step up beside me.

"Cool. Let's make this interesting," says Felix. "You two are on opposite teams. Cavan, you're on the blue team, new girl, you're on red."

"By the way, my name is Kinsey," I call after him as he starts to walk away.

"Okay, folks," says Mr. Calabiner as he forms a line between the two teams by laying jump ropes on the ground. My teammates include Felix, two boys that are snickering about something and a few girls who look like they don't really want to be here. The only person on Cavan's team that I recognize is Zoey, the girl who insulted me on my first day. Via is cheering us on from the sidelines. Mr. Calabiner finishes laying out the jump ropes and brushes his hands together. "Nobody can cross this line, or else you will be disqualified."

Ms. Betta, my history teacher, walks over with a bag full of balls. She starts placing them along the line. "On the count of three, we'll start. Three... two... one... GO!"

At that, everyone beelines for the balls. I whip my head around frantically, unsure if I should battle the crowd to get a ball or not. Before I can decide, a kid that I don't know darts past, his shoulder slamming into me and shoving me headfirst into the grass.

What a great start.

Before I do much more than look up, there's a ball flying at my face. I roll out of the way just in time and scramble to my feet. The ball lands beside me and I pick it up.

I look around for someone on the other team to throw it at, but with everyone running back and forth like chickens with their heads cut off, it's impossible to aim at one individual person.

Every few seconds, Ms. Betta disqualifies players by shouting their name. "Ramirez, you're hit!" "Smith, you're out!" "Peters, didn't you feel that ball hit you in the face? You're out!"

Before long the amount of players in the game has been halved. And somehow I'm still standing. Actually, 'standing' isn't accurate. I've ducked and dodged all kinds of balls by dropping to the ground, diving out of the way and jumping into the air. I still haven't hit anybody, unless you count that one pedestrian. Hey, in all fairness, walking right by a seventh grade dodgeball game is a dangerous move.

As the game progresses, I begin to notice that people aren't trying to hit me as much. I assume it's because they don't see me as a threat, and so they're ignoring me and trying to eliminate the people on my team who are better at the game. Maybe if I continue to fly under the radar, they'll all eliminate each other and then I'll win. It's worth a try.

I walk around aimlessly, pretending to look for a ball. Nobody notices me, which means my strategy is working. I do this for the rest of the game, until the only people left are Felix and I for the red team and Cavan and Zoey for the blue team. I watch Cavan walk over to Zoey and whisper something to her. I can't hear what he's saying but I see him point at Felix, who's jogging over to me now.

"We need a strategy," he pants as he bends over, breathless from running. "Any ideas?"

"Um… here's one," I say. "How about we both try and hit Zoey?"

"Why Zoey?" asks Felix. "I think we should both try to hit Cavan because he's faster."

"But Zoey's hit more people," I say. I don't actually know if that's true, I'm just trying to come up with an excuse to keep Cavan in the game. Maybe that way one of us will win the stone.

"Good point," says Felix. But just as he's turning to walk away, a ball comes hurtling out of nowhere and conks him in the head. "Oww!" he growls. Then, realizing that he's out, he stomps his foot and storms off the field without another word.

I whip my head over to the other side of the field. Zoey has an evil expression on her face and a ball in hand, poised to throw it.

I look to Cavan for help. He points to a ball in front of me and mouths *throw it*. I shake my head because I'm more likely to hit the moon than Zoey. But Cavan just nods until I finally sigh and pick it up.

Not really trying, I toss the ball across the field. It doesn't hit Zoey. Not immediately, anyway. I watch as the ball bounces off a tree, soars through the air and ricochets off a street lamp, flies back and hits Mr. Calabiner in the back of the head and finally soars straight at Zoey. She squeals and throws her hands in front of her face just as the ball hits her.

"Zoey, you're out!" Ms. Betta calls out. Zoey scowls and walks away.

That leaves just Cavan and I. I walk up to the line that separates the two teams and beckon him over.

"You can just throw a ball at me and then we'll get the stone back," I tell him, stepping back. I spread out my arms in surrender.

And that's when people start chanting. It starts with one person, then all of the other seventh graders join in. "Face off! Face off! Face off!"

"It looks like they want a show," says Cavan over the obnoxious chanting.

I sigh in exasperation but realize that if one of us has to get hit, then we should at least make it look real. I smirk as I bend down to grab a ball. "Then it's a show they're gonna get." I chuck the ball at Cavan, who drops to the ground just in time to dodge it. He gives me a competitive look as he picks up the ball and hurls it back at me. I drop and roll to avoid it.

I stand up and before I have a chance to realize what's going on, there's another ball flying at me. Two thoughts flit through my mind in the millisecond before the ball connects with my head: *I don't have time to dodge it. I'm going to get hit.* And then one last one: *I'm not going down this easily.*

Suddenly, I feel my feet leave the ground. Before I can even realize what's happening, I'm doing a backflip in midair. And even more miraculously, I land on my feet.

I just stand there, so shocked by my own actions that you could knock me over with a feather. Never in my life have I been good at gymnastics. As far as I know, I don't even know *how* to do a backflip. Let alone one as flawless as that one. *What is going on??*

Everyone is staring at me. I can tell even without looking. Cavan is, too, but he snaps out of it and throws another ball at me, presumably as a test. I spring off the ground and do some sort of crazy twist in the air that I normally wouldn't attempt in my wildest dreams. I land just as gracefully as last time.

"She's cheating!" one kid calls out.

But how can I be cheating if I don't even know what I'm doing?

Cavan picks up another ball and throws it at me. Still not fully in control of myself, I jump into the air and perform some sort of aerial twist. But while I'm upside down in midair, I grab the ball that Cavan threw and lob it back at him. When my feet hit the ground, I'm standing backwards, so I whip back around just in time to hear Ms. Betta shout out, "McAuley, you're out. Everdell, you're the   winner,   that's   enough   showing   off."

Felix brings over the stone and drops it into my hands. I'm still in complete disbelief over what just happened, but I manage to forget about it at least temporarily when Via and Cavan rush over to me.

"We have to save Ricky," says Via immediately. She takes the stone and flips the date to say, '*Mesozoic Era.*' We all grab onto the stone.

"Everyone, prepare yourselves for complete and total chaos," says Cavan, and we all disappear.

A Journey Through Time

I land on a pile of dead leaves, which disperse as we all hit the ground. Immediately, the sound of screaming fills my ears.

I get up and look around for the source of the ear-piercing shouting. As I expected, It's Ricky. He's standing about ten feet away from where we are now, so I rush over to him, Via and Cavan at my heels.

"Ricky! What is—?" I start. He points with a trembling finger up to something above us. I follow his wide-eyed gaze up until I see an enormous orange beast that looks remarkably like a T-Rex. Holy moly, it *is* a T-Rex!

Time is frozen as the four of us just stand there in silence, staring up at it, too shocked to speak. "Run," I manage.

And just like that, everything unfreezes. I turn on my heel and run as fast as my feet will carry me in the other direction.

Via, Cavan and Ricky match my pace and run alongside me, panting. The dinosaur's enormous footsteps thunder behind us, each step causing the ground to quake. Our feet crunch on the dead leaves littering the ground as we dash through them.

Beside me, Cavan glances over his shoulder. "It's gaining on us!"

Still running, Via whips out the stone and starts rapidly swiping at the numbers. The dinosaur's head swoops down, mouth open in an attempt to swallow us whole. Since she's too focused on the stone and doesn't realize what's happening, I grab Via's wrist and pull her out of the way, swerving to the side of the path.

The dinosaur roars in frustration and tries again. But this time, its aim is dead on, and it's too late for us to try to dodge it. Ricky screams at the top of his lungs.

I shut my eyes tight and instinctively throw my hands over my head. At the very last second, right before we're about to become dinosaur meat, Via seizes my wrist and we disappear.

When we reappear, we're laying on what seems to be gravel. "Where are we now?" I ask, because it's definitely not the dodgeball field.

I stand up and look around. We seem to be in some sort of battle arena—a circular cement wall with lots of arch-shaped windows surrounds us. It looks a lot like…

"The Roman Colosseum," Cavan murmurs, looking around.

"It can't be. Pinewood Falls wasn't built in Rome," says Via. "We were in Pinewood Falls when we teleported. We can only time travel to that exact spot."

I pick up the stone off the ground and examine it. The date says 72 AD.

"Uh, guys…?" says Cavan, fear etched across his face. "I think we have bigger things to worry about." He points ahead. I pry my gaze from the stone and turn my head to see a man wearing a heavy-looking metal helmet with a bright red plume and carrying a short, sharp-looking sword.

Ricky gasps and staggers backward when he sees the gladiator. "We're all gonna die," he whimpers, then turns to us, a stern expression on his face. "But if we do make it out alive, you guys are going to have some serious explaining to do."

"Not now, Ricky," I growl when the gladiator steps forward and starts circling us.

"Hold on!" Via says desperately. "We're not your opponents. Don't hurt us."

But the gladiator just keeps walking around us, ignoring Via entirely. "He can't understand us," says Cavan. "The Romans spoke Latin, not English."

I bite my lip and we all step back until we're pressed up against the wall. The gladiator keeps circling us. "What do we do?" I mutter.

"Use the stone!" Via hisses. Oh, right. I pull out the stone and start flipping the numbers behind my back so that the gladiator doesn't see it.

And then, Ricky steps forward. In a loud, confident voice, he says, "Listen up, gladiator man. On't-day ill-kay us-hay or-hay else-hay ou-yay ill-way e-bay orry-say!"

Everyone is silent for a second. "That's Pig Latin, you moron!" Via growls. Ricky deflates a little and shuffles back over to us.

It's been almost 15 seconds since I changed the stone's numbers. I make sure that Via, Cavan, Ricky and I are all touching for when we teleport.

The gladiator strides over to us and prepares to strike with his sword. "Come on, stone!" I mutter, willing the stone to hurry up and teleport us. Just as the gladiator raises his sword, we disappear and fall into a different year.

The ground we land on is bright white and cold as ice. The harsh wind smacks me in the face and makes my eyes water. The blizzard around us blows powdery snow in all directions and makes it so that I can barely see two feet in front of me.

"Are we in a blizzard?" someone shouts, and I think it's Cavan, but I can't tell because I can't see him.

"I think so!" I yell.

"But how? It's supposed to be summer!"

I carefully try to stand up, but the ice underneath me is too slippery. A sharp gasp escapes me as my knees give way and I hit the ice elbow-first. A searing pain shoots up my arm when I try to put weight on it. *That's going to leave a mark,* I think as I slowly try again to stand up.

"We have to g-get out of here! It's f-freezing!" someone shouts, and I think it's Ricky this time.

"Does anyone have the stone?" I call. Nobody responds. "Everyone, look for the stone! It has to be around here somewhere!"

I use my hand to shield my eyes from the storm and scan the ground for the stone. Ricky's right; we *do* need to get out of here. We're in the middle of a blizzard and we're all wearing t-shirts and shorts. So yeah, it's pretty cold.

"I found it!" Ricky hollers. "What should I change the number to?"

"Don't change it until we all find you!" shouts Cavan.

"Uh, sorry dude, it's too late," says Ricky.

"Ricky, say something!" yells Via. "We'll walk towards the sound of your voice!"

"Uh, okay. SOMETHING!!!!" Ricky bellows. I think I heard it coming from somewhere up ahead, so I walk blindly in that direction. Actually, *walk* isn't accurate. I *slip and slide* my way in that direction.

Before long, Ricky becomes visible through the storm. Then Via and Cavan. We all grab onto the stone with ice-cold hands and disappear.

When we reappear, we're on some sort of orange rock, and the bright sun is blazing hot. "Come on, why aren't we back yet?" Via groans.

I stand up and look around. On one side of me are mountains of orange rock, and on the other side is a giant gaping hole. Wait, a giant gaping hole??

I lurch backward away from the bottomless void of darkness. And then there's a *crack* that makes my insides flip over. "What was—?" Ricky starts, and he doesn't have a chance to finish, because at that moment, the ground falls out from under us.

Before I have a chance to realize what's happening we're all falling down the pit of doom, screaming our heads off.

"Ricky, why did you take us here!?" Via yells.

"I don't knooooow!" Ricky shouts.

The wind whistles past my ears, getting louder by the second. It feels like going down the first hill of a giant roller coaster, only a hundred times worse. I shut my eyes and tense up, preparing to hit the ground.

"Wait! The stone!" Cavan shouts. "If we can find it, then we can teleport before we hit the ground!"

"Does anybody see it?" I ask.

"No! Just a bunch of darkness and—oh, I feel something!" Ricky yells.

"Ricky, that's my hand!" Via barks.

Maybe this valley really is bottomless, because we still haven't hit the ground yet. But I have a sinking feeling that it's only a matter of time before we do. I reach out and feel for the stone, but my fingers grasp nothing but air.

"I have it!" Cavan calls. "Everybody, quick, over here!"

"Over *where*?" Via shouts.

"Over *here*!"

I move my arms forward and back as if trying to swim through the darkness. I reach out and touch something. "Who is this?"

"Me, I think," says Via. "Cavan, is this you?"

"No, it's me, weirdo," Ricky snarls. "Go away."

"Ricky, now's really not the time for this!" Via says impatiently.

"I think I found Ricky," says Cavan. "Is everyone touching each other?"

"Yes!" we all shout in unison. "Now hurry up and get us out of here!" Ricky yells.

"You know, on second thought, maybe I'll just leave you here," says Cavan.

"Take me with you! Take me with you!" Ricky says hastily.

"That's what I thought." There's silence for a few seconds, and then gravity reverses. As usual, we start floating back up, then the blue void, then falling.

We reappear on the old-fashioned floral carpet of a building. "I know this carpet," I realize, standing up. We're in the Dawhill Hotel, right next to the grand staircase.

Then, I hear yelling coming from upstairs. The sound is muffled by the walls, so I can't make out what people are saying. I listen as a door slams and footsteps pound down the staircase. Tiffany storms down the steps, arms crossed. She looks *livid*.

Without so much as a greeting, she rages, "My parents are so unfair. They don't even care about this hotel, they just care about the money. They treat their employees, including me, like absolute *garbage*. I'm sick of it. I wish this hotel never existed."

She flings open the hotel doors and stomps outside. I wait until she's out of earshot to say, "Well, that was strange."

"I know," says Via, looking concerned, "but we really have to get back." She holds out the stone and changes the date back to 2023. We all grab ahold of the stone.

This time, when I hit the ground, prickly grass tickles my arms, the hot sun is beating down on me and the scent of freshly-cut grass fills my nostrils. Relief floods me and I stand up. "We're back!"

"Okay, you guys have some serious explaining to do," says Ricky. "What in the universe was all that?"

Via, Cavan and I exchange glances. Via sighs and holds up the stone. "Ricky, if we tell you what just happened, you have to promise not to tell a soul."

"Sure, whatever," says Ricky carelessly.

"This stone can take you into the past," Via explains. "Whatever the numbers on the stone spell out, that's the year that it will take you to."

"Oh cool. Well, bye, losers." Ricky leaves us and dashes over to Felix. I listen to him say, "Hey, Felix, you'll never guess what those losers over there can do…"

"Remind me to never tell him anything," Via sighs.

"Okay, seventh graders! Time to walk back to school!" Mr. Calabiner shouts.

"If anyone asks, today never happened," I say. Via and Cavan nod.

*   *   *

When I walk into my house, Mom walks over to me, looking happy. "How was your last—" she starts, but cuts herself off with a gasp. "What happened to your arm?"

I look down at my arm and realize that slipping on the ice earlier left a pretty decent bruise. I laugh sheepishly. "Intense game of dodgeball."

"Do you need some ice? I mean, it looks pretty painful—"

"I'm fine, Mom," I assure her, and head up the stairs to my room.

Later, the sky is dark and I'm flopped across my bed, turning the stone over in my hands. I don't understand how earlier, we time traveled back to Rome and into the middle of a blizzard and onto a cliff when we started in Pinewood Falls and it's currently summer. Usually, you can only time travel back to that exact spot and day of the year, just a different time in history.

My thoughts are interrupted by footsteps on the wooden staircase. Will steps into my room, carrying his stuffed dinosaur, Ropher at his heels.

"Hi, Kins, what are you doing?" he asks before I can hide the stone.

"I'm, uh…" I think about lying, but reconsider. If Ricky, of all people, knows about the stone now, then why shouldn't my own brother? "Can you keep a secret?"

Will nods eagerly.

"Have you ever wanted to see a dinosaur?"

A few minutes later, Will, Ropher and I sit on the edge of a cliff that overlooks a lush forest. Pterodactyls glide through the star-pricked sky and the heads of tall T-Rexes poke out from the trees.

"Whoa, look at that one!" Will exclaims, pointing at what seems to be a brachiosaurus moving slowly through the trees.

Ropher, who's sitting on my lap, barks at the dinosaurs. I laugh. "Ropher, I'm pretty sure you don't want to pick a fight with one of those things, buddy."

"Look! It's a triceratops!" says Will, his legs swinging back and forth over the edge of the cliff. Ropher barks at that one too.

It's nice to have something to take my mind off of the Dawhill for once, but in the back of my mind, I know that time is ticking. We only have two days to figure out who burned down the hotel, and then it all goes down. Which means that we really have to get working to solve the mystery.

But whatever happens, we will have tried our best to save the hotel, and that's all that matters.

At least, that's what I keep telling myself…

The Stone of the Past

The next morning, even before the sun has fully risen or the dew on the grass has evaporated, we meet on the porch of Via's house.

Ropher's nails click against the wood of Via's porch steps as I lead him up. Mom thinks I'm taking him for a walk, so he'll be tagging along with me today.

"Tomorrow is the burning of the hotel," I say, plunging my hands into the pockets of my windbreaker as the cold morning breeze blows my hair behind me. I glance up at the cloudy sky—it looks like it's going to rain.

"I know," says Via, worry tinting her expression. "We have to find who did it today or else we'll ruin our chances of saving the hotel."

"We'd better get looking, then," says Cavan. "1987?"

I nod and pull out the stone. I swipe my finger along the numbers and change the date to 1987. I pick up Ropher, and we all hold onto the stone and disappear.

I actually land on my feet this time. I'll take that as a good sign. Taking a hold of his leash, I set Ropher down on the dirt path and we start walking towards the Dawhill wreck.

"I don't see why we came back here," says Via. "There's nothing left to see, we've already investigated the wreck so much."

"We've only investigated it from the outside," I tell her, letting Ropher off his leash so that he can run around. I stroll back over to the pile of wood and prepare to climb it. "Who knows what's on the inside?"

"Kinsey, I don't think that's a good idea," Cavan says nervously as I tentatively set my foot on a wooden plank, testing to see if it's sturdy.

"Yeah, you could get hurt," Via warns.

"I'll be fine." I grunt, grasping a long metal rod and hoisting myself up to the top of the pile. I carefully stand up on a charred wooden floorboard to get a good view of the wreckage. There are tons of wooden planks, all blackened and burned to a crisp. I spot what seems to be a chunk of the ornate floral carpeting, but most of it is completely singed so it's hard to tell if that's what it really is. There's lots of burnt metal, including a fancy curtain rod that's bent at an odd angle. It's hard to see all of this stuff that was once displayed inside a beautiful hotel in a state like this.

"What do you see?" Cavan calls.

I start to cautiously walk around. "Noth—" I start, but cut myself off with a sharp gasp as my foot falls through a gap in all of the wreckage. I hook my arms around a piece of wood and pull myself back up.

"Are you ok up there?" Via asks.

I force a laugh. "Uh-huh, just tripped."

I continue searching the pile for something that could help us. Out of the corner of my eye, I see something glinting in the sunlight. I carefully make my way over to the object, which turns out to be a pearl necklace with a fancy silver pendant. Somehow, it's completely unharmed, unlike the rest of the building. *I've seen this necklace before,* I think. And then it hits me.

"It's Tiffany's locket," I murmur.

"You don't think…?" Cavan trails off.

"No. No, it can't be," I say, shaking my head in disbelief. "Tiffany's so nice. So innocent. She would never do something like this."

"The more I think about it, the more it makes sense," says Via. "When we see her, she's usually upset about her parents. About how they don't actually care for the hotel, just the money that it brings them. And just yesterday when we saw her, she stormed off and wished that the hotel never existed."

"But how could someone so young pull off burning down a whole hotel?" I ask, searching for a reason for it not to be true.

"Her age could actually be an advantage," Via explains. "Nobody would suspect an innocent little thirteen-year-old girl."

As much as it pains me to admit it, it does make sense. I grit my teeth, stuff Tiffany's locket into my pocket and climb down from the wreck.

"Tomorrow, we'll stop Tiffany and save the hotel," I tell Via and Cavan firmly. Via nods and pulls out the stone. I scoop up Ropher and we travel back to 2023.

When I get back to my house, I immediately walk up to my room and pull out my notepad to write down some notes on Tiffany.

Before my pen even hits the paper, Mom calls me. "Kinsey, we're going to the library to get some books for Will. Want to come?"

"Sure," I shout. They might not have had any books on magical artifacts at the *school* library, but maybe they'll have something at the *town* library. Maybe I could even find out how we time traveled back to the middle of a blizzard and all of the other random places. Or how I did those crazy gymnastics tricks during the dodgeball game. It's worth a try, so I follow Mom and Will out to the car and we drive to the library.

When we step into the library, the scent of old books combined with a hint of vanilla greets us. The town library is about ten times as big as the school library, with tons of rickety wooden bookshelves that stretch from floor to ceiling. It's so quiet that you could hear someone turn the page of a book from across the room—quite literally.

"I'm going to take Will to the kids' section," Mom whispers. "Feel free to look around."

Mom and Will stroll off to the childrens' aisle and I'm left to my own devices. I look around the library, thinking.

If I were a book about magical artifacts, where would I be?

Usually, when I walk into a library, I seek out the nearest fiction aisle and head straight towards it. Would magical artifacts be considered fiction? Not if they're real.

I decide to ask the librarian at the front desk. When I approach her, she glances up from her book and gives me a 'you're-wasting-my-time' look.

"Um, excuse me, do you have any books on magical artifacts?" I ask.

At that, her expression changes. Her lips purse into a tight line and I catch her glance at a leather-bound book behind the desk. She looks back at me and feigns an overly cheerful smile. "No, we don't. Sorry, dear."

"What's that book over there?" I ask, gesturing towards the book behind the desk.

"What book?" asks the librarian, not even taking her eyes off me.

"Er—the one behind the desk? You just looked at it a second ago?"

"I don't know what you're talking about," says the librarian. She still hasn't looked away from me or even blinked, and it's starting to freak me out a little. Abruptly, she stands up, chair legs scraping the ground. "Well, it's time for my lunch break."

Just like that, she walks right out the library doors. *That was weird,* I tell myself. My eyes wander over to the strange book on the desk.

There's nobody watching me. I know I shouldn't, but it's just too tempting. Looking over my shoulder to make sure nobody can see me, I reach over the desk and pick up the book. I tuck it under my arm and speed-walk away from the desk, sitting down at the first empty booth that I can find.

I set the book out on the table and read the title. *Mysterious Artifacts.*

Jackpot, I grin, opening the book. I flip the yellowed pages to the table of contents and run my finger down the list until I find *The Stones of Power, Pages 89-90.*

That sounds promising, so I turn to page 89. The text is divided into multiple columns, each one with a small sketch and a heading like 'The Stone of Invisibility' or 'The Stone of the Past'. I eagerly read that section.

"'The Stone of the Past is a legendary artifact that has so far only ever been found by me, the author of this book,'" I quietly read aloud. "'It's incredibly difficult to find, because it is found in the mouth of a gargoyle statue that changes locations almost daily. When unnaturally vibrant blue lightning strikes a building, the gargoyle appears inside, and will remain hidden in the building for approximately 24 hours. Then it will disappear, lightning will strike a different building somewhere in the world, and then it will teleport there. That is, unless someone happens to find the statue and remove the stone from its mouth. Then it will remain there for until the finder chooses to put the stone back.

"'If you stumble upon this stone, it will take you back to whatever year you change the numbers to spell out. Say, if you change the numbers to spell out '1-6-4-8', then you will be taken back to the current time in the year of 1648. Just make sure not to drop the stone on the way to the past, otherwise you will be stuck there forever.

"'One odd thing that I have discovered about this stone, as well as the other stones of power, is that if you are touching it for a certain amount of time, some of its power may seep into your veins and grant you some sort of abnormal ability. For me, it gave me the ability to talk extremely fast without stuttering. Strange, but interesting.

"'Something else that I've discovered about these stones is that if the weather is extreme, they could start to malfunction. For the Stone of the Past, it may start to take you to completely random places around the world at completely random times. I was taken to a volcano when I was trying to use the stone in the middle of a blizzard—that was not pleasant.

"'After learning all about the stone and its abilities, I returned to the gargoyle statue to investigate it. I found small dials on the tips of each of its wings. One was to change the month, and the other was to change the day. By placing the stone in the gargoyle's mouth and changing the dials to whatever day of the year you'd like, you can teleport to exactly that day and year.

"'If you happen to find this stone, my one piece of advice for you is to *be careful*. Time travel is dangerous. Serious consequences come to those who meddle with the course of history. Do not use this stone if you don't know what you're doing.'"

I close the book, feeling a rush of excitement. "Oh, wow. This is a huge discovery! I have to tell Via and Cavan!"

"Shhhh!" the librarian at the front desk hisses, oblivious to the fact that the book is missing.

I clamp a hand over my mouth and laugh sheepishly. I grin down at the book.

"It looks like the hotel was burned down around 9 p.m.," says Via over the phone later that night.

"So we'll meet in front of the school at that time tomorrow," I confirm, sliding the curtains of my bedroom window shut for the night.

"Maybe we should get there slightly earlier, so that we can catch Tiffany before she burns down the hotel," Cavan suggests. "Does 8:30 work?"

"Sure," I say, climbing into bed. "See you then."

"Bye." We all hang up and I click off my lamp. I lay flat on my back, staring up at the ceiling as thunder grumbles outside. I could try to sleep, but it would be no use. Tomorrow is a huge day.

No, it's not a huge day, I tell myself. *We'll simply travel back to 1986, find Tiffany and tell her not to burn down the hotel and everything will be completely fine.*

Famous last words?

You got that right.

CHAPTER TWELVE

The Burning of the Dawhill Hotel

Before I can even blink, I find myself on my bike, riding to the school. The sun is setting behind the trees, giving the sky a warm orange hue.

This is it, I tell myself, bowing my head against the wind and squinting down the deserted road. *We're going to change history and save the hotel.*

My tires glide through a puddle of rainwater, spraying a refreshing mist over my legs. The school comes into view up ahead and I pedal faster.

I hop off my bike and balance it on its kickstand when I reach the front entrance of the school. Via is already here, sitting on one of the metal benches on the side of the walkway, biting her lip and fidgeting with her fingers. She stands when she sees me.

"Are you sure you want to do this?" she questions. "I mean, what if something goes wrong and we end up trapped in the fire or something?"

"It'll be fine. Trust me," I assure her. "We'll travel back to 1986, tell Tiffany not to burn down the hotel, and then leave. We'll be completely fine, and so will the Dawhill."

The whirl of bike tires sounds from my left. Cavan dismounts from his bike, leans it against the brick wall of the school and walks over to us.

"Ready?" he asks.

I nod confidently, pulling out the stone and changing the year to 1986. We all place a hand on it.

"Just remember, whatever happens, we will have tried our best to save the hotel," says Via. "And that's all that matters."

I feel my feet lift off the ground, and then I'm falling through the endless blue void. I hit the ground, facing the star-flecked night sky.

When I stand up and brush the dirt off my legs, I'm relieved to see that the Dawhill is still standing. The street lamps illuminate the space in front of the hotel, and I immediately spot Tiffany leaning against one of them. She's looking down at the ground, her arms folded. Does she look like she's about to burn down a hotel? It's hard to say.

"There she is," I whisper out the corner of my mouth to Via and Cavan. I tread over to Tiffany, who looks up when she hears my footsteps.

"Oh, hello, Kinsey," she says casually. Acting natural. Nice move, Tiffany.

"Hi, Tiffany," I say. "So what are you up to?"

"Not much," she sighs, looking up at the moon. "And you?"

"Nothing suspicious. Aaanyways, what are you doing tonight?"

I expect her to react and admit that she's going to try and burn down the hotel, but she doesn't. She just stands there and doesn't even flinch. "I don't know. I'll probably go to bed soon."

I try to hide my confusion. "Um. Okay. You're not planning on... I don't know... burning down the hotel?"

She looks at me sideways. "No…? Why would I do that?"

"No reason." I give her a quick wave and hurry back over to Via and Cavan.

"Well?" Cavan asks expectantly.

"She's either not going to do it, or she's really good at keeping secrets," I reply, glancing at her over my shoulder. She doesn't look very suspicious at all.

"Maybe you made her change her mind," Via guesses. "Now we can—"

But she cuts herself off with a yelp. At that moment, I feel a pair of ice-cold hands close around my arms. I whirl, and my eyes go wide when I see who the cold hands belong to.

Edward, the unicorn hunter. The one who used the stone to travel into 1986.

"Well, well, well, if it isn't the kids who ruined my life," the hunter snarls.

I whip my head back to see that Frank and Fred, the other two hunters, have ahold of Via and Cavan. They seem to have their cloaks back, even though we took them. "Wha—? How did they get here?"

"A hunter never reveals his secrets," Edward smirks. At that, Frank and Fred start cackling like hyenas.

"Whadda we gonna do wid' em', boss?" Frank asks.

Edward tilts his head thoughtfully, his tight grip on my arms not budging. "Hmm. How about we take them to the attic while we decide?"

I freeze and my heart skips a beat. *The attic?* Tiffany said that room is known for having bad things happen inside. I don't know what kind of bad things, but I know I don't want to be a part of them.

Frank and Fred nod vigorously. Edward pulls me towards the doors of the hotel, and I try to break free of his grip. "Let go of me!" I growl, but Edward doesn't budge.

The hunters drag us up the stairs and up to the attic. The wooden floor creaks under our footsteps. The attic is empty except for three chairs that stand back to back in a circle in the center of the room. The only light is provided by two lit torches perched on the walls.

Edward shoves me back into one of the chairs and pulls a roll of thick rope out of seemingly nowhere. "Let's tie 'em up while we go discuss what to do," he rasps. He starts unraveling the rope, and wraps it tightly around me and the back of the chair while I just sit there helplessly. He ties the cord behind me and brushes his hands together as he steps back, admiring his work. "This shall do."

Frank and Fred finish up tying Via and Cavan to the chairs and scurry after Edward as he flounces out of the room, his dark cloak billowing behind him.

I wait until the hunters are out of earshot to talk. "What do we do?" I ask frantically.

"It's not like we can escape. These ropes are *really* tight," Via grunts.

"If I die, tell my dog that he's a very good dog," says Cavan. "Oh, and tell my cat that she's an… um… okay cat!"

"If *I* die, make sure my parents give all of my stuff to charity and *not* to my sister!" Via says hastily.

"Nobody's going to die!" I growl impatiently. "We just need to find a way to get out of here!"

"Like what?"

"Um…" I scan the small room for something useful, and my eyes land on one of the torches. "There. We'll kick a torch off the wall, hold it with our feet and use it to burn through the ropes."

"But then we'd burn ourselves, too," says Via. Even though I can't see her, I can tell she's smirking. "How about we throw it at the hunters when they come back in? I'd love to see those dumb cloaks of theirs go up in flames."

"That could work," I decide. "We'd have to get closer to the wall…"

I jerk my body to the side, and the chair scrapes against the floor, scooting slightly closer to the torch. Via, being closer to the torch than Cavan, mirrors my actions.

"We'll catch it together," says Via once we've scooted close enough to the torch.

"On the count of three. One… two… three!"

I kick the torch and it goes flying out of its slot on the wall. Via and I catch it with our feet and balance it there.

"I don't think this is a good idea…" says Cavan.

"It'll be fine." I turn my gaze to the door and wait for the unicorn hunters to arrive. "Any minute now…"

I hear footsteps clomping up the stairs. "Get ready to throw it," says Via.

As soon as Edward makes it to the door, his eyes go wide. "Throw it!" I shout, and the torch goes flying through the air.

Edward lurches backward and my heart drops as the torch clatters to the wooden floor. A flame ignites, and begins to spread across the room.

"Run," Edward murmurs. His cloak flowing behind him, he flees, running back down the stairs.

I watch in horror as the flames spread rapidly across the room, blocking the only exit. It's a miracle that the fire hasn't reached us yet.

"We have to get out of here," I say urgently.

"How?" Via asks, looking to me fearfully. The glowing flames glint in her worried eyes.

Good question. I jerk against the ropes, trying to break free. I lurch to the side, causing my chair to tip and fall to the ground.

I can't get up now. The flames flicker in front of me. My heart pounds like a marching drum and I tense up, preparing for the fire to burn me.

But it doesn't. I open my eyes to see the flames licking the ropes binding me to the chair. *They're going to burn through.*

I watch as the fire blackens the ropes and they fall apart. I pull out of the ropes and scramble to my feet.

By now the entire attic is engulfed in glowing flames— they're all over the floor, the walls and they're even consuming the chair that I just broke out of. Beads of sweat form on my forehead as I bite my lip and untie the ropes on Via's chair with a trembling hand. She shrugs off the ropes and hurries to untie Cavan.

I look around the smoky room and wonder, *how are we going to get out?* There's only a small area that's not on fire, and we're standing in it. The entrance is completely blocked off; there's only a small space in between the ceiling and the fire.

Cavan breaks free of the ropes and we all look around for some way to escape. My thoughts are racing and my heart is pounding. I try to calm myself down by taking a deep breath, but I take in a bunch of smoke and only make matters worse.

"There's no way to get out but through the fire," says Cavan, talking fast.

"Or *over*," says Via. She gets a running start, dashes forward and hurls herself over the flames blocking the exit.

It's the only choice I have. I follow, barreling over the fire and rolling down the short hallway, getting dangerously close to the edge of the stairs.

Cavan comes next, and the three of us bolt down the grand staircase onto the second floor. When we reach the ground, my jaw drops.

The whole hotel is on fire now. Paintings on the wall have fallen to the ground, dismantled by all of the chaos. Smoke fills the room, making it hard to see or breathe.

"We have to get out of here," I choke through a lungful of smoke. We rush down the steps onto the first floor, which is even worse. Flames emerge everywhere, burning anything they touch to a crisp. Smoldering floorboards have started falling from the ceiling, crashing to the ground. Smoke stings my eyes and fills my lungs.

I waft the smoke away from my face, coughing as I stumble towards the front doors. I find that a heavy wooden plank has fallen and blocked off the doors.

"It's blocked," I murmur, the tempo of my heart doubling. I turn back to Via and Cavan, but find that they won't be much help. Cavan is on the ground, a heavy-looking floorboard on top of his foot. I make to rush over and help, but Via stops me.

"I'll help Cavan—" she pauses and coughs on the smoke "—you focus on opening the doors!"

I nod and whirl back around to face the doors, shaking off my sweaty palms. I grip the floorboard and try to pull it out of the way, but it's too heavy and doesn't budge. I try again, but with the weight of the thing coupled with my sweaty, shaky hands, it's no use. I finally try slamming my whole body into it, but that doesn't do anything. It just hurts my shoulder.

This is it, I think. *We're going to die here.*

I've just about given up all hope when there's a deafening *crash*. I whip around in the direction of the sound to find a light too bright to take in all at once. I shield my eyes from the light, and after a second, I realize that it's Pearl. The unicorn that we saved from the hunters, being ridden by a cloaked figure.

I stare for a minute. "Hop on, quick," says the figure, extending a hand. I'm too desperate to care who it is and grasp their hand, pulling myself onto the unicorn's back. Via supports Cavan over to the unicorn and the cloaked figure pulls them onto Pearl's back. There's barely enough room for the four of us, but it works.

Pearl rears and takes off. Weak from swallowing all that smoke, I hold on with all my might to the cloaked figure's shoulders as Pearl gallops straight up the fiery hotel stairs.

Pearl crashes through the roof of the attic and soars into the night sky. I breathe in about a gallon of the fresh outside air, still drenched in sweat and trembling from all the craziness.

Now that I finally have a chance to think, the truth hits me like a thousand bullets.

It was us.

We burned down the Dawhill Hotel.

Somewhere In Time

I can't sleep. I didn't expect to, with all of the thoughts racing through my head. I lie awake in bed, staring at the ceiling,

If we hadn't tried to save the hotel, then it would still be standing, I think. If we hadn't wandered down that forbidden corridor and found that gargoyle statue, the Dawhill would still be standing. If I hadn't moved to Pinewood Falls, the Dawhill would still be standing.

If you think about it, it's all my fault. I'm the one who got us into this mess in the first place. I suggested that we try and save the hotel, so it's my fault that it was burned down. It's my fault that my friends had to go through that. Because of me, Via got in trouble with her parents and Cavan broke his foot.

I feel awful. If only there were some way to fix this.

Is there?

My eyes wander to the book that I picked up at the library sitting on my desk. Didn't it say something about a way to time travel back to whatever day you wanted?

I throw off the covers and tiptoe over to my desk, careful not to wake Mom or Will. I sit down and flip the pages of the book to page 89, sliding open my desk drawer and pulling out a flashlight. I click the flashlight and hold it a couple of inches away from the page, quickly finding the sentence that I was looking for.

"'After learning all about the stone and its abilities, I returned to the gargoyle statue to investigate it,'" I read to myself in a hushed tone. "'I found small dials on the tips of each of its wings. One was to change the month, and the other was to change the day. By placing the stone in the gargoyle's mouth and changing the dials to whatever day of the year you'd like, you can teleport to exactly that day and year.'"

As a plan starts to form in my mind, a random memory pops into my head. When we were first figuring out how to use the stone, we traveled to 2022 and Via met her past self. It changed the course of history.

I grab my phone and text Via and Cavan.

Meet me in front of the school at 6:30 tomorrow night. Via, bring your mom's keys to the building.

I climb back into bed, smiling. Maybe there's still a little hope left after all.

*   *   *

The next night, I sit on one of the metal benches by the entrance to the school, fiddling with Edward's cloak in my hands. I've brought it with me, just in case. I hear footsteps and turn to see Via and Cavan approaching, Cavan limping with a bulky-looking boot on his foot. Via doesn't look very happy, but she's carrying a ring of keys, so I'll take that as a good sign.

She glances at the stone in my hands and looks at me with an eyebrow raised. "You really want to use the stone again? Even after the mess it's gotten us into?"

"I know," I say. "But just hear me out. I have an idea that just may get us *out* of trouble. We'll have to go back to the gargoyle statue, though."

Via raises the keyring she's holding. "We're going to break into the school?"

I open my mouth to protest, but change my mind. "Technically, yes, but it's for a good reason."

Cavan falls onto one of the benches, clearly exhausted from walking all the way here with a broken foot. He sighs. "Why not? It's not like we could make this any worse than it already is."

Via still looks unsure, but finally gives in and shakes her head. She strolls over to the doors and slides her mom's key into the lock. There's a click, and she pulls the door open. We step inside the deserted building.

When the door swings closed behind us, darkness closes around me like a fist. "I knew this would happen," I murmur, plunging my hand into my pocket and whipping out a small flashlight. I click it on, illuminating the space ahead of us.

I navigate through the dark, empty hallways until we reach the forbidden corridor. This time, I don't hesitate before strolling down the hallway, Via and Cavan following closely behind.

When we reach the gargoyle statue, I discover that its mouth is still hanging open, just waiting for the stone to be placed back inside.

I spin around to face Via and Cavan. "Okay, so here's the plan. We're going to go back to June 2nd, 1986, and stop *ourselves* from burning down the hotel."

Via frowns. "I don't know, Kinsey. It's really dangerous. You were in that hotel last night while it was burning to the ground, what could possibly make you want to go back?"

"It's our fault that the hotel was burned down, and we need to make it right," I say confidently, pounding my fist into my open palm for emphasis. "This is the best way."

"But June 2nd was yesterday," says Cavan. "Won't we have to wait another year before we're able to go back?"

"Actually…" I turn to the gargoyle statue and stand on my tiptoes to reach the tips of the wings. Sure enough, there's a small dial on each of them. The one on the left says *June* and the one on the right says *3*. I swiftly swipe the dial on the right wing so that it says *2* and place the stone into the gargoyle's mouth.

Then, the ground starts rumbling. I step backward as all of the cracks in the concrete statue flash bright blue, just like the eyes did on the day we found the stone. The light gives the dark hallway a vibrant blue glow.

"I think we have to grab onto the statue!" I shout, placing a hand on one of the gargoyle's claws. One hand holds the statue while the other grips the three unicorn hunters' cloaks. Via and Cavan grab on just in time.

There's a blinding blue light, and then a grinding sound that makes my teeth clench. I feel my feet rise into the air, then I'm once again falling from a dark night sky. I hit a grassy ground with a *thud.*

I stand up and instantly feel a rush of déjà vu. The Dawhill Hotel stands before me. Tiffany is leaning up against one of the street lamps that provide a warm light to the otherwise pitch-dark parking lot.

And there's someone walking up to Tiffany. She has dirty-blond hair and is wearing the same t-shirt and shorts that I was yesterday. Wait. I think that's—

A hand seizes my arm and pulls me back into the woods. "What were you thinking??" Via hisses. "You could've seen yourself!"

"Well, we'll have to eventually *talk* to our past selves," I remind her. "Speaking of which, we should do that now."

I turn back towards the hotel, but Past Me is nowhere in sight. *What happened after I talked to Tiffany?* I look around the area, and find myself talking to Past Via and Past Cavan off to the side of the parking lot.

I start to walk over there, but stop in my tracks when I see three people in dark clothes approach our past selves. It's the unicorn hunters. I bite my lip and fight the urge to look away when I realize it's too late. Past Via yelps, and it's only a matter of time before the hunters drag us away.

Once the hotel doors slam shut, I tread back over to Via and Cavan, starting to panic.

"It's too late," I tell them. "We already went inside."

"Well, why don't we just follow us inside?" asks Via.

"The unicorn hunters are in there," I say, glancing back over my shoulder as if maybe this time things will be different and we'll escape the hunters' clutches. It doesn't seem likely. "If they see us, they'll think we escaped and bring us back to the attic." I stifle a laugh as I imagine the hunters' faces when they see double of each of us.

"Uh, guys? Look," Via says, gazing up at the top of the hotel with an alarmed look on her face. I follow her gaze up to the attic to see thick black smoke pouring from the roof.

I stand there helplessly, staring up at the attic in horror. A glowing flame appears in the window, and then the attic bursts into flames. Blackened pieces of wood and siding fall from the building and plummet down to the ground.

Our past selves must be at least on the second floor now. Maybe even the first. And once we reach the first floor, we search for a way to escape, but the door is blocked by a wooden plank. And then, Pearl the unicorn comes crashing through the wall to save us.

Speaking of whom… I look around the hotel and in the woods for Pearl, half expecting her to come barreling out of the forest and charge head-on into the wall of the hotel. But she's nowhere to be found.

I wait for a minute, but there's still no sign of her. Via frowns uneasily at the burning hotel. "We're dying in there."

My mind wanders back to the cloaked person riding Pearl last night. I was too frightened and desperate to make it out of that building alive to even care who it was.

But when I glance down at Edward's cloak in my hands, all of the pieces click into place.

"I know what I have to do," I say determinedly. I pull the hunter's cloak over my shoulders, tug the hood over my head and look around in the woods. A faint glow in the distance makes up my mind for me and I dash in that direction, hurtling through the trees.

I find Pearl standing in a clearing in the forest, her snow-white coat glimmering in the moonlight. She turns to me and cocks her head to the side.

"Hi, Pearl, I need your help," I mutter vaguely. Her periwinkle-blue horn glows in reply. I swing myself onto her back and give her a soft kick in the side. She takes off galloping back through the trees and the burning Dawhill Hotel comes into view.

The wind whistles past my ears and my cloak blows behind me. One hand holds onto Pearl's neck and the other holds my hood in place on top of my head. As we approach the hotel, I duck my head against the wind and prepare to crash through the wall.

Pearl continues speeding across the Dawhill parking lot, straight towards the side of the hotel. I squeeze my eyes shut.

With an explosion of shattered wood and clouds of smoke, we're in. The burning lobby is just as I remember it from last night, planks falling from the ceiling and everything ablaze. And there, right in the middle of it is me, covered in ash and drenched in sweat.

"Hop on, quick," I say, extending a hand. Past Me stumbles over and takes my hand, pulling herself onto the unicorn's back behind me. Then come Past Via and Past Cavan. I pull them up onto Pearl, make sure that everyone is settled, then turn to the grand staircase. I narrow my eyes up at the stairs ahead and give Pearl a kick in the side. As she gallops up the stairs, Past Me death-grips my shoulders with shaky hands.

Pearl crashes through the ceiling of the attic and we soar into the starry night sky. The sound of blaring sirens cuts through the silence of the night and I look down to see dozens of fire trucks pulling up to the hotel. Firemen pour out of the trucks and before I can even blink, the fire is out.

I push lightly on Pearl's neck, sending us gliding gracefully back to the ground. We land a good distance away from what used to be the Dawhill Hotel, but not too far to smell burnt wood or see the smoke drifting from the wreckage.

Past Me, Via and Cavan slide off the unicorn's back, all of us looking equally miserable. I watch us walk away and take out the stone with defeated looks on our faces.

Present Via comes racing over, Cavan limping closely behind. "What happened?" Via demands.

I grin and glance over my shoulder at Past Us just as we all disappear. I hop off of Pearl's back. "I was the one who saved us from the fire last night."

"Wait. The cloaked person riding Pearl?" Cavan asks, his eyes widening in disbelief. "That was *you?*"

I nod, still smiling. But that smile falls when I realize that we didn't accomplish our goal of saving the hotel from ourselves.

"Maybe history just wasn't meant to be changed," Via says thoughtfully, turning to the hotel as the firemen rush inside. "And we may not have saved the hotel, but we did save *ourselves* from a burning building. And that's saying something."

I smile. "Yeah, I guess so."

Then, a new voice besides the shouts of the firemen drifts to my ears. I turn in that direction and find a tall man in a fancy suit talking to Tiffany's parents.

"That's the mayor of Pinewood Falls," Via mutters. We all proceed to eavesdrop on their conversation.

"...It's such a tragedy," I hear the mayor saying. "The Dawhill was such an incredible hotel. It definitely deserves to be rebuilt sometime in the future."

Tiffany's mom scratches her chin, thinking. "Well, when we do, I think we should definitely rename the hotel. The name 'Dawhill' will bring back too many bad memories of tonight."

"How about we call it… the Parkonsville Hotel?" Tiffany's dad proposes. "It is our last name, after all."

"Perfect," says the mayor. "We'll begin construction on the Parkonsville Hotel in a year or so."

"The *Parkonsville Hotel…*" Cavan repeats. "Where have I heard that name before?"

Via gasps, her eyes bright. "Oh! I know! It's the most popular hotel in Pinewood Falls in 2023. It's still standing, even in the present!"

"Whoa," I murmur.

Cavan checks his watch. "It's getting really late. We should get back soon."

I pull out the stone and change the digits back to 2023. We all hold onto the stone and travel back into the future, landing by the entrance to the school.

"I've got to go," says Via. "See you guys soon?"

I pause. "Actually, how about we walk together this time?"

And so the three of us set out under the moonlight, with no plans to travel into the past. From here, the only way to go is forward.

Three Months Later

My mom sits me down at the table, smiling that huge smile of hers. "So, your birthday is coming up," she says. I nod, waiting for her to continue. "What do you want to do?"

I tilt my head back and pretend that I haven't been thinking about this for the past three months. "I'd like to go the Parkonsville Hotel."

Mom looks at me sideways. "You want to stay at a hotel?"

I nod firmly. "And I'd like to bring two friends."

Before long, Via, Cavan and I are walking up the walkway to the entrance of the Parkonsville Hotel, dragging heavy suitcases behind us. "I can't believe we're actually here," Via says in awe, looking up at the huge hotel.

When we step inside, a red-haired woman at the front desk greets us. She seems to be the manager of the hotel. As Mom checks us in, I read her nametag. *Tiffany*.

Tiffany squints at us. "You three look… familiar," she says.

Cavan shrugs. "I don't know what you're talking about."

Then we walk away, following Mom and Will to our room.

Our stay at the Parkonsville Hotel ends up being a blast. We visit the waterpark, spend a night at the arcade, and eat in the fancy dining room.

It's a lot like the Dawhill, but better. The staff seems much happier and so do the customers. It's also a whole lot more fun, with the additions of the waterpark and arcade.

And though it may be called the Parkonsville Hotel, it'll always be the Dawhill Hotel in my heart

Acknowledgements

Special Thanks:

Thanks to Mom and Dad, for taking all the time to read, edit and format this book. Thanks to Grandpa, for being the first one to read this story after I finished the first draft way back in May of 2023. Thanks to all my family and friends and anyone who read this book before it was finished. And, as always, thanks to all of our amazing pets: Sam, Arlo, Bartlet, Simon and even Celeste. Thanks to Amanda Tuttle, for always helping with my book covers.

Final Manuscript Line and Copy Edits: Jessica Smithers, Jason Smithers

Cover Art: Generated by Jason Smithers using Midjourney

Cover Design and Type: Amanda Tuttle

ABOUT THE AUTHOR

Maci is a five-time self-published author. At the age of eight, she told her parents that she wanted to write and illustrate a book. Her parents explained to her that if she learned to do every single part of the process (storyboarding, writing, illustrating, page layout, choosing fonts, etc.) along with her dad, then they would help self-publish a book. She finished the process in 3-4 months with her first picture book titled *Maci and Addie's Fairy Adventure,* followed by her second picture book *The Portal.*

During the challenging year that was 2020, when most kids were faced with adversity, ten-year-old Maci harnessed her creative spirit (and extreme boredom) to complete the initial installment of the series, titled *Ally Lancaster & The Enchanted Fortress*, marking her third literary endeavor and her inaugural novella. Two years later, at the age of 12, she completed the sequel, *Ally Lancaster & The Gemstone Sirens.* While working on finishing up *Ally Lancaster & The Gemstone Sirens*, Maci toyed around with an idea for a middle-grade time travel mystery, which turned into her third novella, and the book you are holding, *The Stone of the Past.*

Thank you for supporting young, independent authors like Maci.

www.ingramcontent.com/pod-product-compliance
Lightning Source LLC
Chambersburg PA
CBHW031156010826
48971CB00012B/739